VAMPIRE GIRL 6: UNSEEN LORD

KARPOV KINRADE

DARING BOOKS

http://KarpovKinrade.com

Copyright © 2018 Karpov Kinrade
Cover Art Copyright © 2018 Karpov Kinrade
ISBN-13: 978-1-939559-51-7

~~~~~

Published by Daring Books

~~~~~

First Edition

~~~~~

🌸 Created with Vellum

This book would not be possible without two special people. Ariz Brune for being the bestest beta reader ever, and pinch hitting the impossible!

And to the estimable Elise Kova, for pushing me to write ALL THE WORDS every day! When you light a fire, it burns, baby.

xoxoxo Lux & D

IRIS

This isn't what it looks like. I swear. You see, though I may be shackled to a cave wall that makes the Black Lotus prison look like a five star resort, and yes, though my blood might be used to annihilate all of humanity by giving vampires free reign over all the worlds, I am in complete control. Utter domination. You get the picture. So, don't worry. All children and sensitive souls may read on.

But what's the plan, Iris, you might be asking.

That's an excellent question. The first part of my plan is to wrap my head around the total plot twist I was just thrown by my childhood hero. I'm the Unseen Lord?

Mind = blown.

I'm also trying to wrap my head around the fact that said childhood hero is sitting right in front of me, shackled just as I am, and in need of a serious bath.

I'll tell you this… when you go to sleep at night hoping and praying to all the gods that may or may not give a shit that you'll get to meet your hero someday, be more specific than I was.

Cuz this ain't how I imagined meeting the great Arianna

Spero, Midnight Star of Avakiri, High Queen of Inferna. I saw this going down verrrry differently. So remember: details matter.

But here we are. There's no avoiding that. Unless someone's got a time machine they could lend me for a quick sec?

No?

Alrighty then...

That's unfortunate. Because the next part of my plan is to bury the pain of seeing Elias die. I'm gonna bury that shit until it grows into a mother effing Rage Tree. And that tree is going to tear Arias to pieces and suck his marrow as a snack.

You know, as soon as I figure out how to get out of here.

Minor details.

The final part of my plan is basically to escape, free the queen and find Aya... yada yada yada. You get the idea. Easy peasy. No problemo.

"I have so many questions," I say to my cell mate.

She nods, her listless, knotty hair flopping in her face. Girl's gonna need some seriously deep conditioning when she's outta here.

"I wish I had more answers," Ari says.

I can see in her eyes that her heart is broken. Her son is dead. Killed by her other son, whom she thought was dead for most of his life. Her kingdom is in ruins. Her legacy collapsing. And I was her last hope.

Good job, Iris. You really nailed this one.

"I'm getting us out of here," I declare with a confidence I'm totally not faking. Not even a little.

"I believe you," the queen says, and she almost sounds like she means it. That's good. We can work with almost.

"How did you end up here? And where's the king?" In the stories, King Fenris never leaves the queen's side. They are inseparable.

"I received a message, inviting me to a meeting to learn

more about my son. About Arias," she says, her voice cracking. Likely she hasn't done a lot of talking lately. Except in my head, but I don't think that exercised the vocal chords much.

"Let me guess, it was a trap."

She nods. "I was arrogant. I became too used to my power and couldn't imagine someone could strip me of it so easily. Even my Spirit dragon, Yami, was captured and imprisoned, though I don't know where."

"Shit. He captured you *and* your dragon? How?"

"I let my guard down. When I saw him, all I could think about was the fact that my son, my baby, was alive. He used a powerful binding spell on me and entrapped us both with trimantium. When I woke, I was here. I don't know what happened to Fen. I just hope he's okay."

I hope so too, for everyone's sake. "So, what do you figure the rider wants with me, the oh-so-evil Unseen Lord?"

"I…"

Her voice falls away as he enters the chamber.

The earth shaking under his heavy boots. His white armor a dark gray in the dim torch light. The rider.

His eyes fall on the trimantium shackles that bind my bloody, chafed wrists, engraved with runes and adorned with scarlet gemstones that block my renewal. He smirks, and I see Elias in that face. That smile. That raised eyebrow. It makes me want to gouge out his eyes.

He turns his attention to Arianna, moving toward the queen with no preamble. Steady, measured strides. He lifts his right hand above his shoulders, slowly drawing the massive sword that hangs strapped across his back.

"You don't need to do this, Arias," the queen says, panicked. "We meant you no harm. You had died. You were checked over by several of the best healers. I don't know

3

what magic brought you back, but we had no idea what we'd done until it was too late."

"I believe you," he says. "But it doesn't matter. Your sin wasn't in thinking me dead. Your sin wasn't in burying my body. Your sin was in burying my name. My existence. In catering to the whims of the superstitious, you ruined what could have been. You ruined my life."

Arianna drops her head forward, her shoulders slumping as tears fall down her cheeks. "Do not ruin the world for my mistake. Please. I beg you."

Arias just shakes his head, moving closer to the queen with a cruel smile on his face.

The queen shrinks away from him, into the shadows, but she can't get far.

"Leave her alone! Deal with me!" I shout, but he ignores me and continues focusing his attention on his mother.

When he's within arm's reach of her, he swings the heavy hilt of his weapon and knocks her over the head. With a sickening crack she slumps to the ground, her new wound seeping fresh blood into the earth.

"Matricide isn't a good look on you," I say, trying to control my breathing and my impotent rage.

"Oh, she's not dead, just unconscious. I needed a private moment with you."

"So why not just take me elsewhere? You don't think you've tortured her enough?"

The Rider shrugs. "These caves are special. Lined with trimantium. You two are filled with the world's most powerful magic. I need a safe place to keep you. Sorry if the accommodations aren't to your liking."

"You could definitely do with some better housekeeping," I say dryly, hoping he's telling the truth and the queen is indeed still alive.

I squint my eyes, trying to discern the outline of her body

through the darkness. It might be my imagination, but did she just shudder slightly? Was that a breath? I can't really tell, but I hold onto the thought nonetheless. Because, like, what else can I do, right?

"What do you want? Why am I still here?"

He approaches me, but stays out of arm's reach. Smart man. I may be shackled and magically powerless, but that doesn't mean I'm without tricks up my sleeve. I trained in many forms of combat in some pretty brutal circumstances. Uncle Sly wanted to make sure I was ready for anything. Child Protective Services could have had a field day with my upbringing, were they ever made aware of its nature. But the magical community has always remained separate from the rules of humans. After all, we need to be ready to deal with things that most humans can't possibly comprehend. So, in that, I don't blame my uncle, and on some days I'm even grateful.

If the Rider would come just one step closer, this might be one of those days.

But he stays in his shadows, watching me closely.

"He's not dead," the villainous man finally says.

"What?" I've lost track of our conversation, clearly.

"Elias. He's not dead. I should have ended him. Had every right to. But I didn't. I called Aya and she got there in time to save him, as I knew she would. I'm not the monster you think I am, Iris. And I need your help."

I respond by spitting the biggest phlegm bomb I can muster into his face.

He sighs and wipes at it with his sleeve. "Really? How juvenile, even for you."

I shrug. "I use the tools I have at my disposal. I'm resourceful that way."

The Rider steps closer, then bends onto his knees. Small shafts of light illuminate the white armor he wears, even here, draped with long strips of cloth to give him the look of one who has risen from the dead to haunt the living. Not so far from the truth as it happens.

"There's more going on here than you understand, Iris. The stakes are higher than you can imagine. I've done what I must for the greater good, and I need your help."

"Why would I ever believe a word you say?" I ask. "You wanted to kill me. You've kidnapped me. Chained me. Done the same to your own mother. And I don't believe for a second that you're telling the truth about Elias." Though damn, I want to. I really, really want to. My heart constricts at the very thought the prince might still be alive, but it's only wishful thinking. The fanciful thoughts of a desperate woman clinging to lies.

"What if I can prove it?' he asks. "Will you help me then?"

I pause. If Elias is alive, that does change things. But not everything. "There's still a lot of bad blood between us, dude. Almost killing your brother isn't something to brag about. And the rest of the list is pretty damning."

He sighs and stands, pacing the cave. "Will you at least hear me out? Listen with an open mind?"

I grit my teeth, angry at my weakness, but finally I nod. "Prove he lives and I'll listen, but you're unlikely to change my mind about anything."

"You're the Unseen Lord," he says.

"Yeah, I got that." I roll my eyes, hoping he can see through the shadows.

"Then perhaps you have heard of the magical chords that connect all those who know the truth about the first vampire. About you."

I nod. "Right. Lix Tetrax. So?"

"So Elias is part of those chords. Part of an intricate pattern of energy spreading throughout all the nine worlds. And you are at the very center, my dear hunter. If you focus,

6

you can ride those chords and connect to him. You above all will have more power to make those connections than even the most skilled of the Unfettered or Lix Tetrax, because the magic began with you. You *are* the chords"

My eyes widen and I sit back, leaning against hard stone as the full impact of what he's said hits me. "So I can connect to anyone who's part of this magical bond?"

"Yes," he says. "Though it has limits. It's not a location beacon. They won't know where you are, and you won't know where they are, not specifically."

Damn. He read my mind. I guess my easy rescue plan is out. Ah well. This is still useful. I will find a way to make it even more useful with time. But first, I need to see if he's telling the truth. I need to find Elias. Assuming this asshole isn't just feeding me a pack of lies.

The Rider turns from me. "I'll come back later, when you're ready to hear my side of the story."

Once he's gone, I let out a breath I didn't realize I was holding.

This is utter shit. He's trying to trick me, and I will not allow myself to be made a tool by this... well, tool.

I know what you're thinking. I should definitely not trust the bad guy right? I mean, he's the villain. He's a liar just based on archetypes alone.

Believe me. I've already considered every way in which this situation could go sideways. Every way it could lead to the ultimate doom for everyone. When you're rotting in a dungeon, those thoughts are easy to come by.

But as my new cellmate would say, if she were, you know, conscious. *Dum spiro spero.* That's old white dude speak for, 'while I breathe, I hope.' Last I checked, I'm still breathing. And so is the queen, I'm pretty sure. So you know what that means, little birds? I'm still hoping.

In fact, remind me to have that phrase tattooed to my

backside when this is done. So when I tell Arias he can kiss my ass, it's not only a solid burn, but also inspirational.

And so, with that hope, I figure there's nothing to be lost by trying what he suggests.

I mean, sure, maybe it's some trap to capture my soul for all eternity, but that seems a little far-fetched and also, why? He's already caught me. It does make me wonder why he needs me to agree to help him. He didn't seem to have that problem before. What changed?

Well, other than me actually being the Unseen Lord and not just someone standing in the way of him getting to the big UL.

I'm probably not what he was expecting. I'm not what *I* was expecting, for that matter.

Okay, enough internal chit chat. If Elias is alive, I need to find him. Stat.

Without knowing what the hell I'm even doing, I close eyes and position my legs and arms into the best lotus position I can given the chains restricting my movement. *Inhale. Exhale. Inhale. Exhale. I am one with the universe and the universe is one with me. Ommmmm.....*

Yeah, this shit isn't working.

I was not designed for meditation. I'm more a doer than a... than a non-doer. I guess? I don't know. I just need an ass to kick or something.

But I shake out my arms and try again.

I'm not thinking of the way my feet are going numb in this position.

Or the itch on my nose.

Or the creepy crawly that's found a good spot on the back of my neck.

Nope. Not thinking of any of that. I am totally focused on...

What? What am I supposed to be focused on? Clearing

my mind? That's not going to work. If my brain were a computer it would have a hundred tabs open and something really big trying to download on a slow wi-fi.

So I need a focal point.

Duh.

Elias, of course.

I think of Elias. Of the way he smiles, and the way his eyes dig into mine as if he can read my thoughts. The way he smells... like a forest of fresh leaves and pine. The way his body feels against mine when his arms are wrapped around me.

And bam! Just like that, I'm in.

I feel him, his body, his essence, everything about him flows in and around me. "Elias!" I scream his name, desperate for him to hear me, to know that I'm alive and okay. Relief floods me as I feel his pulse increase, as something in him jerks at the sound of my voice in his head.

And then I'm pulled out, just as fast, like something sucked me back into my body. My skin is slick with sweat and my muscles shake from the effort. A pounding headache makes me extra unhappy as I peel open my eyes.

I slump to the side, vomiting the nothing that was in my stomach. Bile and some acidy shit I probably needed. When my dry retching is done, I lay my head on the cold stone and try to calm my breathing.

That wasn't fun.

But it was fruitful.

Arias wasn't bullshitting me. Elias *is* alive.

And he's worried about me.

Desperate to know where I am.

I could feel that much.

He's also in danger. I could feel that too, but I don't think he realizes it. I'm not even sure how I know this. I just do.

I have to get out of here and help him. I have to warn him.

In the corner of the cave, the queen stirs, moaning as she tries to sit up.

I scoot over to her, ignoring my spinning head, and rip a piece of my shirt to hold against the wound on her head. "Arianna, are you okay?"

She moans again.

"Elias, he's alive! We have to get out of here and help him. You have powers," I say, tying the makeshift bandage so it will stay on its own. "What are you able to do?"

The queen rights herself against the stone wall and holds up her feeble, shackled wrists, bruised and crusting with blood. "My powers are spent, what little I had. I'm afraid I'm of no more use to either of us."

I sigh and lean back on my heels.

"What do you mean Elias is alive?" She asks. "How do you know?"

"It comes with being the Unseen Lord," I explain. "I can sense him. Feel him. And he's in danger. We have to get out of here."

She nods, and a look comes over her face that sends pin pricks of warning over my skin. But before I can react, a sound like a demon being tortured hurtles out of her mouth and she lunges for me, wrapping her chains around my neck. "You will die. You must die!"

Her voice doesn't sound like her, and wow but she's got more upper body strength than I gave her credit for. Woman must do Pilates or something. Being completely unprepared for the attack, my response time is slow as the chain tightens around my neck and her knee finds its way into my kidney. But it isn't until her teeth sink into my neck and she begins to drain me of my blood that I realize too late she could actually kill me.

And this time I won't come back.

ELIAS

*H*er face is hard. Serious. The look of a warrior. But I will defeat her. I shall prevail. In this and in all things, just you wait.

You believe me don't you? You haven't lost faith in me since nearly being killed by the White Rider? I didn't think so.

She lunges, I parry, then counterattack, our swords clanging against one another, metal ringing out in the cool night air, the sound reverberating over the icy waters that surround my sister's ship. In the distance stand the snow-laden mountains of Stonehill, replete in their quiet, sparse beauty. The parts of my childhood I remember most fondly all happened here.

"Lighten your grip," Uncle Asher instructs, as if I'm a child still learning the art of war through play and wooden swords. It is only the three of us aboard just now. The rest of her crew members have taken to Uncle Dean's realm for a night of debauchery and pleasure. Aya said they needed to let off steam. I personally think she just wanted to be rid of their boorish company for a spell. I don't blame her.

"Control your hips," Uncle Asher says, continuing his unnecessary instruction as Duke, my black wolf, sits at his side watching with impartial eyes. He's grown monstrously big in such a short time, a sign he's got some of the magical qualities of his father in him.

"They're telegraphing your moves," Asher says. "Aya could defeat you blindfolded with the way you're fighting today."

I purse my lips against a sarcastic retort. The truth is, I'm slower than I should be. Still weak from nearly dying at the hands of my evil twin.

If Aya hadn't come, if she hadn't gotten there in time, all would be lost.

But here we are. I am nearly returned to normal.

Nearly.

But not quite.

And I am distracted by worry for Iris.

I should be out there looking for her. Assuming she's even still alive. Aya doesn't disagree, but she wants me at my best before we venture forth into a fight with a tremendously powerful man.

The White Rider.

Myth. Legend. Blood.

"You're fighting like a blind turkey," Uncle Asher says, as he crosses his legs and sips at a goblet of fresh blood. He's impeccably dressed, as always, hair oiled down, nails polished. And he's been shadowing us for days, ever since I regained consciousness.

Shadowing us, and hounding us.

Aya takes that moment to use my distraction against me and pins me into a lock that nearly ends our battle, and not in my favor. I twist away and am about to counter with an attack that should turn the tables when my vision goes black and a voice explodes in my head, calling my name.

I stumble and Aya positions her blade against my throat, a gloat on her perfect face, as she relieves me of my weapon.

"Brother, you've lost your touch. You'll need to be better than that to go up against the White Rider."

She saunters away, her dark cloak flowing around her shoulders, as she takes an offered goblet from a servant and drinks deeply.

Duke whines under his breath and jogs towards me, nudging against my legs.

It takes a moment for me to form a coherent thought. "I just heard Iris's voice in my head. She's on this world. On Avakiri, I think. I could feel it. Feel her."

Aya raises an eyebrow at that. "How?"

Uncle Asher clears his throat, his gaze penetrating. "Likely something to do with her emerging powers as the Unseen Lord I would think. She is valuable but dangerous. She must be protected."

I nod, glad we agree on that at least.

But he's not done, it seems. "First, however, it is vital we secure the line to the throne and place a new monarch. Your parent's will is clear. They do not have to be dead, just unable to perform their duties, and their title would pass to the next in line. After a vote by the people."

Aya purses her lips. "It should go to the oldest, as is custom."

Uncle Asher inclines his head. "Be that as it may, it is not how your parents wrote their will. I was there when they commissioned it. It was a compromise between your mother and father. The vote would be limited to their royal line, but would be voted on by the people. A balance between the rule of monarch your father desires and a rule of democracy your mother prefers."

Aya wrinkles her nose, scoffing at the notion. "This isn't Earth. We can't employ their government styles here, and honestly, their ways aren't working well for them either. I know my mother is well-intentioned, but in this she is wrong, and she has made my father weak. Inferna needs a strong queen who will rule justly but also fiercely. So much more can be set right with a strong fist than a soft heart."

I shift uncomfortably and let my hand fall to Duke's head, giving him a distracted rub behind the ear. Politics was never my forte, and I was never the favorite of the royal children. "Look, I'm fine with Aya taking this on. I'd be a shit king and we all know it."

Uncle Asher's face is unreadable, but I know he has thoughts he will share later. He always does. "You do yourself, and the people of Inferna, a disservice, nephew. I know you had challenges growing up, but you also have an inner strength that would lend itself well to the ruling of this kingdom." He stands, setting down his goblet. "At any rate, the point is moot. The instructions are clear. We must move forward with the choosing of the new monarch before we embark on any rescue mission."

Aya and I exchange a glance. But really, she shouldn't worry. There's no way in hell—pun intended—that they'll vote me in as king. It will never happen.

We make our way by boat to Uncle Asher's kingdom of Pride, where he instructs a series of letters to be sent to his brothers. "The realms must be notified. This time tomorrow we will have a great ball at High Castle. Each realm must send in votes by proxy with their representatives. Within each realm there will be feasting to celebrate the crowning of a new king or queen."

The scribe nods and hurries off to do his bidding, then he looks at us. "You both must prepare yourselves. I will have my tailor commission for each of you something splendid to wear. For one of you will be crowned tomorrow."

The door to the study opens a crack and Varis walks in.

The man towers over most, and stands out with his bald head covered in tribal tattoos. An owl perches on his shoulder, his Druid Spirit that he is never without. He approaches my uncle and lays a hand on his shoulder affectionately. "You are needed. A villager has come with news about Fen and Ari."

"What have they to say?" I ask.

Varis regards me with unreadable eyes. The Druid has been with my uncle since before I was born, but he has always been an enigma to me. "I don't know the details. They would only speak with Prince Asher."

Uncle Asher leaves with his partner, but turns before exiting. "I will tell you anything I learn. In the meantime, get fitted and then get some rest. Tomorrow everything changes."

* * *

The fitting is tedious, but over quickly enough—Duke sleeps through the whole thing, lucky him—and Aya slips away after, claiming she needs some time alone. Though we grew up together, nearly inseparable, I've always found her a hard person to read. She keeps her cards close to her chest, as it were.

Late that night I seek out my uncle to discover what the villager had to report. I find him with Varis in their personal quarters, each of them stretched before a fire reading leather bound books. The scene is so domestic, so comforting, that it makes me long for something I fear I'll never have. I've been on the run for so many years, living in makeshift spaces, doing what I could to infiltrates the shadows of Lix Tetrax and the Tempest, that it is strange to be home, to be back in what was once so familiar.

My thoughts turn to Iris and I begin to wonder if maybe

this kind of life could be in the cards for me after all. Would she want this? I honestly have no idea. Our relationship is too new. We haven't had a chance to discuss what a future together might look like, if indeed there even is one. Would we live in Inferna or at the Black Lotus? I'm surprised to discover there's a part of me what would prefer to come home. Maybe not to take up my role as Prince of Envy's realm. But perhaps to live a quiet life somewhere in the Outlands, free of politics and the machinations of my world.

But how could that ever be? I am too entrenched in the darkness of the Unfettered to ever break free. And I am still on the Council's Most Wanted list. Which makes all of this, particularly me being included for the vote of king, so absurd. I can't very well rule under the circumstances, even if I were the better choice, which I clearly am not.

I push away such thoughts and sit next to my uncle at his beckoning.

He sets aside his book to look at me. "The news was nothing. A villager who wanted the reward money but had little to offer for it. Just rumors of your mother being in Avakiri, but nothing concrete. I am sorry."

I don't school my look of disappointment fast enough and Uncle Asher puts a hand over mine. "We will keep looking. We will find your parents," he says.

"And Iris," I add.

He nods. "And Iris."

I want to ask more questions, to probe him further about what he knows of the Tempest, the White Rider, my parents, the Unseen Lord, but we've already been round and round with that conversation and he will likely be as tight-lipped now as he was then. I'm confident he knows more than he's saying, but I'm just as confident he'll only tell me if and when he feels like it.

So I bid them both goodnight and head back to my room, Duke at my heels.

My sleep that night is restless, and the next morning we leave for High Castle, to begin preparations. It's a flurry of activity, with servants cleaning, polishing, cooking, basting, baking, trimming, and decorating. My uncle's tailor must have worked non-stop since the fitting, employing some magical help, no doubt, because by the afternoon both Aya and I are decked in the finest silk, satin and velvet.

"Do you really think it's a good idea to parade me around when I'm still the Most Wanted of the Nine Worlds?" I ask Uncle Asher, as he supervises while his tailor dresses myself and my sister like dolls. Even Duke gets a brushing and a dignified collar for the occasion. I would have thought he'd hate it, but he takes to it like Uncle Asher would, prancing around showing everyone how handsome he is. Silly wolf.

"Nonsense. The only ones who care about that blasted list are council members and Hunters, none of whom will be here," he says.

"Not even Thalius?" I ask. "He's keen to see my head on a spike, and has blood bonds to both Avakiri and Inferna, making this election of interest to him."

My uncle just smirks. "I've ensured Thalius will be unable to attend. Worry not, dear nephew."

Aya raises an eyebrow at that, but then flinches and becomes distracted as her gown is tightened around her waist. "I do need to be able to breathe. Please keep that in mind," she barks through gritted teeth.

Once dressed in the finest fabrics of deep purple, gold and black, we join Uncle Asher in the throne room, which is presently void of all but a few guards standing at the ready. "Your uncles will be joining us, then we shall commence with the voting, ceremony, and festivities. Each realm has already been celebrating all day, so everyone is in fine spirits."

I'm sure that's not true. Not everyone cares about which spoilt Royal sits on these thrones. Some are just trying to survive. Some are enduring discrimination by the vampires, the Fae or both, if they're unlucky enough to be Shade. My parents have done their best, but you can't quickly eradicate prejudice. Maybe we can't rid ourselves of it at all. I've begun to believe it's an inherent part of us all, whether we choose to admit it or not.

Uncle Dean arrives first, surprising us all by being fully dressed. "Too cold out there for you?" I tease.

He laughs in good spirit. "Just enjoying the new silk shipment I got in," he says, running a hand along his intricately embroidered gold tunic.

Aya greets him with a mischievous grin and hug. "Good to see you. Have my men been behaving themselves?"

Uncle Dean smiles and shrugs. "Nothing my people can't handle." In many ways he is the opposite of Uncle Asher. Where Asher is polished and poised, with dark hair and pale skin, Dean is debonair and casual, dark blond hair wild, skin sun-touched. But they are the closest of the brothers. I often noticed my father watching them wistfully, perhaps pondering missing memories of the times they had before he was turned. Memories he lived many lifetimes thinking were his until he found out the truth about his heritage, that he was never born a vampire under the curse of the seven sins, but rather was Fae, touched by the Druid Spirit, who nearly died during the battles until the vampire queen, my grandmother, turned him.

It's a story no one really talks about, but I did get it out of my mother once. She was always more likely to tell us the things others wanted to stay hidden.

Pity she didn't tell us about my twin.

Uncle Ace arrives next, looking slightly distracted and anxious, like a mad scientist who can never quite master the thing he wants the most. "I'm working on something new," he says as he enters the room. "It could help speed up production of basic household goods, but uh... " he looks down at soot covered hands and shrugs. "There are still some complications to work out."

Dean smiles indulgently. "You'll get it."

"Speaking of inventions," Aya says, cozying up to him. "I need a contraption to take a fleet of ships to Avakiri through the Waystones. Do you think you can put something like that together?"

His eyes light up and he rubs at his stubbled chin. "Actually, I've been working on a design for just that purpose. It's as if you've read my mind."

Aya waggles her eyebrows at me in excitement, presumably planning for the rescue of Iris, which I appreciate, then lowers her head to engage in a low volume back and forth with her favorite uncle. He built her ship, after all. Her prized possession. As a child she spent more time in his realm learning about inventions than in our own. Though she took to our father's combat instructions readily enough, as evidenced by her fame as a fighter.

Uncle Zeb is the last to show, and is decked out in luxurious clothing befitting his title as Prince of Gluttony. Thanks to him we have an incredible feast for this evening. Perhaps the only thing I'm looking forward to in this entire event. He greets the group with a small nod of the head.

Once all have arrived, Uncle Asher stands and produces a contract, signed in blood by my parents. "Our instructions are clear. All heirs of Ari and Fen are to stand before the people of Inferna to vote on who shall become the new queen or king of Inferna. If Ari and Fen return at some future date, and in a condition to resume their previous position, the new ruler will have the option to refuse and stay on, or to acquiesce the throne until such a time that Ari and Fen retire permanently. We have, due to these unfortunate circumstances, triggered this clause, and must now begin the trials to determine the next ruler."

Zeb frowned. "Why are we not eligible for this position? It was, after all, a chance of fate that Fen was Ari's first choice and not one of us. Shouldn't we now have the opportunity to put ourselves in the ring for this role? We who have trained for this position for hundreds of years?"

While Ace, Asher and Dean had been clear allies of my parents during the last war, the stories of Zeb were a little more tempered. He didn't betray them like Levi. But... he was never completely satisfied with how it all unfolded, I think. And Aya is doing a poor job of schooling her face to neutral. She's clearly unhappy with the idea of more competition for the vote. After all, against me, she knows she's guaranteed the crown. Against one of our uncles? That might be a tougher vote.

"While your concerns are duly noted," Uncle Asher says, "this is the way of it. They are the law and they make the law." His tone leaves no room for argument, and I get the impression this isn't the first time the two of them have had this conversation.

Zeb remains silent, and with that bit of family mutiny aside, Asher addresses his brothers. "Do you each have the tallied votes of your realms and any realms you are leading in absentia?"

That last bit is a dig at me, since I should be producing a scroll for Levi's realm, Envy. But I no longer reign there, and the castle has fallen to ruin, though it did produce the Twilight Bow for us, which would have been really useful if we hadn't lost it to the White Rider, and the Moonlight Sword to the Black Lotus. Aya would normally be managing the realm of Greed, but Zeb has brought that scroll on her behalf, while Dean collected the votes for my realm.

They nod in unison and hand Asher scrolls that will decide our fate and the fate of our land.

Asher reads through each, raising an eyebrow at one, until he has memorized the results. He is now the only one in Inferna who knows the identity of the next sovereign of our kingdom. He smirks with that knowledge and escorts us to the balcony where a throng of vampires, Shades, and even some Fae, await below. Two crowns are perched on a red velvet pillow. One for me. One for Aya.

I absently wonder what they will do with the loser's crown.

The cheer of the crowd is deafening as we step out, and Duke presses close to me, always on the look out for enemies. It's late afternoon and the sun is dipping lower in the sky. I've spent so long on Earth, I've forgotten the simple luxury of basking in the warm rays without fear of harm. I let myself enjoy the moment as Uncle Asher waits for the cheering to die down.

"Thank you all for joining us on this most auspicious occasion." Asher is interrupted by more cheering. When it quiets, he continues. "Though the circumstances that brought us here are less than optimal, rest assured the safety, security and prosperity of the realms are our utmost priority, even as we investigate what became of our Queen and King."

The crowd erupts again, and I refrain from rolling my eyes at this pandering to the crowds, which just proves my point that I am truly not cut out for this gig, as Iris would say. The thought of her sends an unexpected pang through me, and I have to force myself to focus on the ceremony taking place.

"After reviewing the results, the will of the people is clear. You have chosen... Princess Aya Vane Spero of Stonehill, daughter of the High Queen and King, as your new ruler."

This time there is no subduing the hysteric clapping, hollering and crying. The people are thrilled.

I expected to feel a surge of relief at not being chosen, and I do, for the most part. But there's also an unexpected emotion buried in my gut I do not quite understand and have no time to dissect now.

It's enough that Aya is glowing with joy and triumph. She will make an excellent leader of our people, of that I feel confident.

So why, I wonder, is that sense of unease in my gut lingering as Asher places the crown on her head?

IRIS

$\mathcal{T}$hey should have just killed me. It might have been easier. I mean, take off the magic blocking cuffs first, then kill me.

People think dying is hard. Nah. Pain is hard. Suffering is hard. The fear of the unknown is hard. Dying is relatively easy, all things considered. Especially when you know you'll come back.

I've died more times, and in more ways, than I can count. Some were painful and gruesome, some easy and painless. None as hard as what I'm suffering through now.

Whatever the Queen of Inferna and Midnight Star of Avakiri did to me, it hurts like a mother effing bitch.

I know you're probably thinking, seriously Iris? You were cooked alive and eaten, and this is worse?

Yes.

This is worse.

Why?

Because I have no control over the situation. I did not choose this. I cannot alter it. I am at the mercy of others. That makes it infinitely harder.

What hurts worse? Ripping off a bandage, or someone else doing it? Someone else doing it, obvs.

When we intentionally choose pain, we are emotionally prepared for it. When it happens to us, we are victims.

That's always harder.

So when I wake, I'm not a happy camper.

I'm in pain.

Miserable.

Half coherent.

But at least I'm not dead dead. For real dead. And I'm not in a filthy cave anymore.

So there's that.

And yes, I realize I'm being a whiny ninny. Just let me have this one okay? I've been through a thing.

As I peel my eyes open, soft light penetrates my vision, but it might as well be the rays of a thousand suns as it pierces my brain and sends shooting pain into my body. My neck throbs and my bloodstream pulses with a kind of ache I've never felt before.

Cool hands press against my throat and a woman's voice mutters words in an ancient language.

"She's waking," a voice I recognize says. "About time. It's been over two bloody days."

"Arias, you mother fu—" I choke on my own words as a flash of electricity zaps something inside me and my body spasms. "What the—"

"Try to control your temper, Watcher. It's not helping," the Rider says with what sounds like some gloat in his voice. Bastard.

The woman's voice pauses and she removes her hands. The ache in my veins fades as her magic pulls away from me.

I try to sit, but the world spins. Strong hands support my back to keep me from passing out again.

His hands.

Double bastard.

Okay yes, I'm feeling very salty right now. Do you blame me?

When the world stops spinning and my vision focuses, I find myself staring into the silver eyes of a blue-haired Fae. She's frowning at me, and there's a strength and intelligence in her face that tells me she's not one to trifle with.

"Where am I?" I ask, bringing a shackled hand to my throat. Checking to make sure it's still there (my throat, not the shackles. Though both are still there...) My fingers worry at two bite holes that are already healing. "And what the hell happened?"

The hands supporting me move as the Rider shifts to stand in my field of vision. "The queen attacked you," he says. "It was my fault. I should not have placed you two so close together under the circumstances. But I didn't expect her to behave like that."

That makes two of us. "What's wrong with her? What have you done to her?"

"He has done nothing," the woman says. "The curse the queen has fallen under is not his doing, but that of another."

"And who are you?" I ask, turning my head to face the woman who clearly had a hand in healing me.

She glances at Arias, who nods, then back to me. "I am his mother."

"His mother is being tortured and held in a cave," I say, still bitter at Arianna's treatment, despite recent events. And we'll get back to that curse statement in a hot sec. There's a lot to unpack here.

Her head dips in acknowledgment, but her eyes stay firm. "I am the one who raised him."

I wrack my brain for more info on her, but what the Rider told me was sparse at best. "What's your name?"

Again, furtive glances between the woman and Arias before she speaks. "Kayla. My name is Kayla Windhelm."

Total jaw drop. Not gonna lie. She has left me speechless with this proclamation. I've thought a lot about what spawned the nightmare that is the Rider, but this... this is... I don't even know. Because I've read my histories. I know the name Kayla Windhelm. And this.... Holy shit. This is intense. "But... you're... you're his father's half-sister. And you were the queen's best friend. How...?"

"All of this is true," she says. "And yet there is more to the story."

My head is spinning from this. "Wait... you said your father was killed," I say, looking at the Rider, who takes a seat next to his mother on a simple wooden chair.

There's a fire crackling behind them, and I realize we are in a quaint cottage that looks like it could be the home of the proverbial witch in the woods. Dried herbs hang from the ceiling, a large black pot bubbles over the flames, and it smells like all manner of medicinal brews. I'm laying on a simple cot.

Kayla hands me a shallow wooden bowl filled with a sludge brown broth. "Drink this. You won't like it, but it will help that headache you have."

I take it and sniff delicately, recoiling at the stench.

She smiles. "It smells better than it tastes, I'm afraid."

That's not great news. Still, this headache is a thing of legends, so I plug my nose and down the concoction like a shot, gagging as I do. I will my body to keep it in, and the Rider hands me a clay mug with water to drown the taste. It doesn't work, but I drink it up anyways and hope the coating on my tongue doesn't outlast my existence, though I fear it might.

It will certainly never leave my memory.

Imagine taking the rotting flesh of a swamp monster and

mixing it with putrid shit of a sick unicorn (and as an FYI, contrary to popular memes, unicorn shit is the absolute worst. Like seriously, worse than any other shit I've ever had the misfortune of smelling). So take all that and mix it with... I don't even know... the intestinal fluid of a demon. You might have an idea of what this was like to drink.

"I'm guessing you don't have a lot of people beating down your door for a taste of this?"

She laughs. "You'd be surprised. It's shockingly effective."

I pause, and then realize I literally feel no pain. Zero. "Wow. You weren't kidding. That shit is potent."

She nods and takes the cup and bowl from my hands as I ponder how I might compel her to give me the recipe. Not that I want to ever smell or taste that demon shit again, but damn it could come in handy in my line of work, ya know?

"So, back to the part where you betray your family and kingdom?" I say, looking to Kayla for answers.

Kayla Windhelm. Legendary blacksmith. And loyal—at least I thought—advisor and friend to the High King and Queen of Inferna. Clearly I'm not up on current events on this world, because holy hell! This is serious.

"She didn't betray anyone," the Rider says, his face hard and defensive. "The royal family is compromised and putting all the Nine Worlds at risk. We need your help."

At this point my stomach decides to make its presence known with a growl so loud a black and white tiger I didn't see until now shifts from the floor in front of the fire and looks up at us, a low rumble building in his chest.

"Is that...?" I look at the beautiful creature and gulp, just as the fur shifts to skin and the feline into man.

"Tavian Gray," he says with a deep voice. He's naked and doesn't seem to mind or care. I turn away, but not before noticing the rich caramel of his skin and finely carved muscles. Averting my attention to his face doesn't help much.

It's just as mesmerizing with green eyes the color of emeralds.

He grins and Kayla rolls her eyes, clearly used to the affect her husband has on others.

"Wait a minute." I turn an accusing look at the Rider. "You said your father was killed."

The Rider shrugs. "He was. Or at least, I thought he was. I ran after that. Left the island thinking it would spare my mother and those I loved from further pain." He glances with an apologetic look at Kayla. "It didn't have the effect I'd hoped."

Tavian shrugs into pants, but doesn't bother with a shirt. Okay then.

"Well, this family reunion has been fun and all, but you still have the queen locked in a cave. You still tried to kill me and your brother. Those things haven't gone away," I accuse him.

My stomach growls again and Tavian moves around the kitchen putting food together while I try not to stare at him.

I'm used to being around immortals. So it's not that strange that Kayla and Tavian look the same age as the man they raised as their son. What is strange is lusting after a legendary figure with his wife right here, also a legendary figure.

But more than that, finding out said legendary figures— who fought and bled for the queen and king—are part of the mystery of the Rider's rise to infamy. Everything feels off in my world now, and I don't know how to make it match up again.

"So... you two are responsible for the king of jackasses, Thalius, and the White Rider plaguing our lands. You must be so proud. Is your next venture a book on parenting?" The sarcasm drips from my mouth, and I'm surprised after my very solid and well-deserved burn that Tavian still deigns to feed me, but I don't object when he hands me a plate of bread, cheese and fruit. I eat it gratefully, not even caring at this point if it's poisoned. I'm too hungry for that to matter. Besides, if Arias wanted me dead, he wouldn't have saved me.

After I've stuffed my face and my belly, the Rider raises an eyebrow and takes a seat in front of me. I don't like playing invalid in bed, so I swing my legs off to the floor and perch sit on the edge of the cot, making eye contact with him. "Better be careful, Rider. I'm still dangerous, even with these shackles."

Tavian chuckles but says nothing, and I scowl at them both. Clearly he wasn't phased by my parenting insults.

"That's why we need you," the Rider said. "You're power-ful. As a highly trained Watcher, but also as the Unseen Lord. I, alone, can't stop what is coming. But maybe with your help, we can."

"And what's coming?" I ask, curious despite myself.

"War," he says. "The likes of which you have never seen."

"Uh huh. This is based on…?"

"The Tempest—the leader of the shadow organization Lix Tetrax, and the one who pulls the strings of the Council of Hunters— has infiltrated the royal house," the Rider says. "We strongly suspect he is behind the bewitching of the queen. I intended to awaken the Unseen Lord to stop the Tempest and his corrupt organization once and for all. I was expecting… "

"Let me guess, not me? Some old wise white dude, perhaps?"

Arias at least has the grace to glance away in shame at that. "Still, you have the power I seek. We need your help."

"For what? And why should I help you?"

"To save this island, for one. And to save the worlds for another."

"That's enough," Kayla says, standing. "She is a stranger. We cannot tell her more."

The Rider huffs in annoyance, and it's such a teenage kid thing to do I nearly laugh. It's surreal seeing the White Rider, the terrifying legend, reduced to being reprimanded by mommy.

"She will not trust us without knowing the whole of it."

Tavian walks over and slips an arm around his wife.

"She's an outsider," Tavian says with a low growl. "This is too risky. We can do this without her. Your plan was foolish and has wrought nothing but pain for all involved. You should not have ventured forth without us."

"One of us had to act," the Rider says. "Someone had to do something. You two just hide away on this island hoping it will all be okay. You don't see what I see. You don't know what the worlds are becoming. And you don't understand the influence and power the Tempest wields. He is a danger to us all. Especially with what we guard. She needs to know the whole of it since her help can no longer be forced."

At this point, I'm super done with being talked over like a piece of furniture. "Um, hello? Yeah, that 'she' you keep referring to is right here. And I *can* hear you."

No one bothers to even glance my way, let alone respond, and I'm really beginning to feel the sharp sting of disappointment that none of my legends have lived up to their promise. First Thalius, then Queen Arianna, now them. How disappointing all my hopes and dreams have been.

But before I can attempt another interruption, the door bursts open and a man in armor holding a bloody sword stands before us, eyes wild. "The island is under attack!"

IRIS

*T*hat got everyone moving. Tavian and Kayla follow the Rider and the soldier out the door, leaving me to fend for myself. Still handcuffed, of course.

I pull myself to a standing position. I'm a little wobbly, but nothing I can't handle.

I don't know what I'm expecting exactly, when I walk out the door, but it's not the tropical paradise I step into. Brightly colored birds dot the deep blue sky that's quickly fading into darkness as the sun sets, large palms sway in a wind that's scented with the smells of ocean, tropical fruit hang heavy in trees spread throughout lush grasslands that lead to a sandy beach in the distance. I can practically smell fruity cocktails and coconut oil in this place, and I kind of fall in love.

Then my own rank appearance pushes into my consciousness and I realize how out of place I look. I'm a mess, my dark hair in tangles around my dirt-smudged face. I'm dressed in literal rags, since I was naked when I was kidnapped. It basically looks as if the Rider cut a few holes in a potato sack and threw it over my head. I don't even have underclothes, which is super refreshing... not. And I'm not even sure all the 'dirt' on me is actually dirt. Some of it smells… suspicious.

Oh, and I'm barefoot.

So yeah, I'm totally ready to take on the world.

Nevertheless, my Watcher instincts kick in.

Pushing past everyone, I make my way to the Rider.

"Where are we?" I ask, wondering if there's a way I can communicate my whereabouts to Elias. If he heard me speak his name, maybe he could hear other things.

"A secret island in Avakiri," he says without further explanation.

I'm cut off from asking more questions by the sound of battle in the distance. Near the shore, guards from the island place themselves between the village and whoever belongs to the massive black ship hovering in a supernatural mist on the water. All of the invaders that I can see are dressed in black, with black masks to obscure their features.

The village is up the slope to the west of us, and I can see Fae running around frantically, grabbing their children, closing shops, locking their doors. The Fae here are caramel-complected with primarily blue and green hair. They dress in light clothing to fit the warm climate. Flowing fabric in bright colors. They are clearly not warriors. Most of them look like they would be slaughtered if it came to it.

Tavian and Kayla exchange a look and she runs towards the village, presumably to help the people evacuate to safety. That's what I would do at least.

And the Rider and Tavian head to the shore, both pulling out swords, ready to fight.

I clearly have no place in either direction, being chained up and unarmed as I am, so naturally I go where the fighting is, because why not, eh?

At the very least, I need to figure out what's going on and how I can help. Regardless of how I feel about the Rider and his family, I do believe the people of this island are innocent and deserve my protection.

When we reach the shore, I expect the men to dive into battle. There are a handful of invaders already breaking through the island's feeble defense, and more coming on small boats, riding silently through the mist like ghosts.

My feet sink into sand so white it's nearly blinding under the sun, and the water is crystal blue, pristine, and so clear I can see the bottom of the ocean, at least until the mist obstructs my view.

In the distance, at the edge of the breaking waves, to the east of the ship, a woman leans against the jagged rocks, basking in the warm rays of the sun. No. Not a woman. Her legs aren't legs, but rather one large fin, which I realize when she startles at the boats approaching land and dives grace-fully into the water, disappearing in the mist.

"You have mermaids here?" I ask as I approach the Rider. To be honest, the only mermaid I've ever seen is Marashpyr, who stays at the Black Lotus frequently.

Arias nods. "They have their own kingdom within the ocean near here and often come to our lands to trade. They're a private people, but so are we, so it works out."

I have a lot of questions, and I wish I was here for other reasons. Reasons that would allow me to explore this hidden culture I'm becoming fascinated by.

The Rider is standing behind his small span of guards, assessing the situation. One jogs over, blood splattered over his breastplate. "Sir, we're losing men and they have rein-forcements. We need help!"

The Rider nods as Tavian shifts into white tiger mode and roars into battle, tearing legs and arms from anyone dressed in the tell-tale all black. But Arias scans the horizon, looking for something else.

"What am I missing here?" I say.

"This is the first time any ship has discovered this island. It's not a coincidence. Something bigger is at play," he says, frowning.

I nod. "You think these goons are a distraction?" I ask. It makes sense.

He raises an eyebrow. "Indeed. And that is worrisome, given the stakes."

"Which are what, exactly? You never did explain that part."

"In due time, dear Watcher. For now, we must protect the village."

I hold up my wrists. "That would be easier if you unshackled me."

"I can't risk you harming my people," he says.

"Why does everyone assume I'm some killing machine? I don't get it. Seriously. I have a code. Name one person I've actually killed," I challenge him.

He purses his lips, but says nothing.

"Exactly. I'm the good gal."

"Good gal?"

"Yeah, good guy is too sexist. I'm not a guy and that shouldn't be a blanket word to cover everyone. We should start calling everyone 'good gal' instead. Well, only the good ones of course."

The screaming intensifies as the battle pushes inland, and Arias frowns and holds up his hands, palms facing the water that comes alive before us, forming a body that slithers beneath the surface. A turquoise sea creature emerges, body covered in iridescent scales that glint in the sun. The thing is huge and I'm pretty sure I'm only seeing part of it. Like the proverbial iceberg, there's a heck of a lot more going on beneath the water, I'm sure.

My heart pounds in my chest and I prepare to fight the

beast if it comes too close to us, but it doesn't make for the shore. Instead, it targets the boats heading for the island.

And it all finally clicks. I can't believe I didn't put the pieces together before. "*You're* the new Water Druid! Duh. Of course. The ice. The powers of the White Rider. You manipulated your control over water to give the illusion of being the creature from legends."

He bows, as if receiving an award. "At your service. Though 'new' might be a bit of a stretch, given the power descended upon me as an infant nearly 100 years ago. Be that as it may, you are correct."

As we speak, the boats carrying more invaders to the shore are smashed into bits by the sea serpent's tail, wreaking havoc on them all before setting its sights on the bigger ship in the distance.

But before the creature makes it there, a figure appears on a rock formation pushing up from the water. He's dressed in black armor with a gold mask, and when the Rider sees him, he freezes. "It's the Tempest," he says. "And he's far too closer to the power source."

Arias runs towards the outcropping of rocks, and I follow at his heels. "What power source?" I ask.

But before I can catch up to him, a scream from behind me pulls my attention. A little girl is being pulled from the bushes by one of the black-clad invaders. She's panicking, trying to fight him off, but she's no match for him. And he doesn't kill her immediately, which doesn't bode well for the pretty child.

I glance at Arias, who is using his powers to ride the waves towards the Tempest. I want to face the Tempest, to find out the truth of Lix Tetrax, but I can't leave this girl to suffer.

So I abandon my path towards the Rider and change

direction, heading for the child who's being dragged towards the village.

As I run, I consider how best to fight with 1: No weapon, 2: No armor or actual clothing and 3: No Renewal.

I know you're worried right now, and you have every right to be. Even I am usually not in this much hot water. (Get it? Hot water? Like that time I was cooked alive in hot water?) Yeah, okay, at any rate, remember. *Dum Spiro Spero.* While I breathe, I hope.

And... I have a plan. Kind of. It's a terrible plan, as plans go. And could end spectacularly badly for me. But I have to risk it, ya know? What other options do I have.

By the time I catch up with the asshole terrorizing a child, he's got some of his buddies involved in the mix, and they are heading for a hut on the edge of the village. It's surrounded by a garden and there are children's toys strewn in front. I'm guessing this is where the girl—who looks to be about seven years old—lives. Probably with her family. Who will now be facing some serious peril if I don't hurry the hell up.

My plan was really more fitting if I was only facing one attacker, but I can improvise. Sure I can. Heck, improvise is my middle name. (Okay, it's really not, but I never ever tell anyone my middle name. Ever. Even Callie doesn't know it. I'm convinced Uncle Sly, who named me, by the way, hated children at the time.)

I get to the hut a few minutes after the invaders have dragged the girl in, and by the screams I can tell they have found more victims. I don't have time for finesse, or to get a better view of what I'm dealing with, so instead, I take the direct approach.

Through the front door.

"Stop! I am a Watcher of the Hunter's Council and I command you to cease what you are doing and surrender immediately."

The scene before me would be comical if there wasn't a terrified family involved. Three invaders all freeze in the middle of tying up the little girl, her mother, and her father. My bet is the father would be killed off fast while they had their way with the females. Or the father would be forced to watch. Depends on how evil these guys are.

Either way, I'm not letting any of that happen.

So, where was I? Oh yeah, they freeze, and then turn slowly to stare at me. And, like, I can't really see their faces because of the black masks, but let's just imagine the looks on their faces, seeing *me* standing there giving orders. Me, in a potato sack, covered in shit, with shackles on my wrists.

One guy actually lets out what sounds like a tortured laugh.

Then the biggest one, the leader, I'm guessing, pulls out his sword and reaches me in two steps. "You'll make a nice appetizer, then, won't you," he says in a super creepy voice.

Okay to be honest his voice is pretty normal, but come on, bad guys (and we'll go ahead and use guys for this because they are in fact male) should look and sound like bad guys. It's a pity, really, that they don't.

"Oh, you won't like me. I'm scrawny and chewy. Likely to get stuck in your throat." And with that, I use my shackles to grab his sword, pulling it in as my knee inflicts the most damage to the bits of him he was hoping to use soon.

He groans and slumps over and I chuckle. "Won't be needing that for awhile now." I give another kick for good measure, as his two friends lunge towards me, swords swinging.

Just what I wanted.

Now this next part… well, it's going to really come down to a lot of luck and some skill. So say a prayer if you're inclined. Or at least, wish me luck.

Cuz I'm gonna need it.

With the mastery of my craft, I throw myself at the first man, positioning my wrist so that they are in the direct line of his blade trajectory.

It happens so fast.

I blink and it's done.

My hands fall from my arms, like mannequin parts that weren't properly installed. I'm in such shock I don't even feel the pain at first. I think everyone in the room is a bit stunned to be honest, as my lifeless bloody hands land on the hardwood floor with a wet thump.

Then the little girl screams, galvanizing everyone into action.

So, the bad news, I'm losing blood fast and the adrenaline won't keep the pain away for long.

The good news? I'm free of my shackles. That was the plan. I can't die until my Renewal comes back to me. For that, I needed the shackles off. There might have been smarter ways to go about this, but none that would have saved this family in time.

And now, for phase two.

I pivot, avoiding a blow to my neck from the pointy side of a sword, as I reach into myself, searching for the spark I learned to recognize as my Renewal.

After my first death, I didn't die again for a few years, but I practiced with it, practiced sensing it in meditation and worked to understand the limitations and nature of it. When Uncle Sly felt I was ready, we began to test my abilities.

By killing me in different ways to see how I would Renew. To see how long I took to recover. To learn how to best gauge my abilities.

It was a strange kind of training. One I didn't talk much about with others. But it worked.

And so I strained to find my center before blood loss or

one of these goons made that a moot point. And... there! Yes. It's back. I know it is.

And just in time.

Because holy mother of all shit balls, the pain has hit. Mayday, mayday, abort! This is awful. What was I thinking? I need to die, stat.

With a howl that could scare a wild bear, I leap at the closest sword, impaling myself on it with precise aim. Gotta hit the heart, or I could just be screwed instead of killed.

With a triumphant smile, I spit in the eyes of the man holding the sword I'm now hanging from, as my heart beats for the last time.

I Renew just outside the hut.

There's a moment of discombobulation that I've gotten used to over the years. The feeling of new skin, as it were, and of being someplace you weren't just a moment before.

But I recover quickly.

I am at full strength. A perk of my Renewal. But I am weaponless, so that will need to be rectified.

The village is being overrun by the attackers. I wish I could save everyone, but first thing's first.

There's a man lying dead on the dirt road, a Fae. By his side is a sword. It's nothing fancy, but it'll do.

I silently thank him, grab his weapon and storm the hut.

"Stop! I am a Watcher of the Hunter's Council and I command you to cease what you are doing and surrender immediately!"

This time I don't even need to see the looks on their faces. The eyes say it all.

The poor family, though, they look ready to pass out.

The three thugs are surrounding my body and one of them is...

"Ew, gross. Seriously? To a corpse. Have some self-respect

man. Or at least some respect for the dead. That's just disgusting."

Before he can say anything, before any of them can say anything, I initiate what I call the Flying Twirl Death, patent pending.

It looks something like this. Imagine yours truly, sword (or preferably daggers, but today it's sword) in hand, turning into one of the pinwheel spinny things, you know the ones you got at fairs as a kid? Only instead of paper or tinfoil or whatever, it's made of blades. Sharp ones.

I mean, right now it's only one blade, sure, but I am spinning so fast that it looks like half a dozen.

And I cut through those bastards before they even have a chance to raise their own weapons.

And by cut through, I mean that literally. Two are completely headless and one would, I guess technically be called 'nearly headless' by certain people.

You get the idea.

Once that's done, I untie the family and check over the girl. "Are you okay? Did the bad men hurt you?"

She shakes her head. "No. But... but... " she sniffles and cries. "They killed you. You're dead. Right there."

She points to my body.

"I know honey, but I have a magical power that makes me very hard to kill. I'm back. And you're going to be okay."

The mom comes to me, her eyes red and swollen. "You saved our lives."

"For now, but you've got to find someplace to hide. More might be coming."

She nods and the dad takes his wife and child in him arms as they leaves the bloody mess that was their living room. I follow them out and search the village, looking for Kayla. I find her fighting a man in black who separated from his crew. It looks like most of the fighting is still on shore. Hopefully the Rider's sea creature thwarted their full force. Behind her are more villagers that she was clearly trying to lead to safety.

The family sticks close to me as we make a dash towards Kayla, who has already killed the bandit by the time we arrive.

When she sees me, she pauses, noticing that my shackles are gone. "How... ?" she starts to ask, but then shakes her head. "Never mind. Doesn't matter."

"These people need a safe place," I say, gesturing for the family to come up. "They're okay, but have been through some trauma."

"We'd be dead or worse if not for you," the man says with gratitude, even as they all shake from the fear and trauma of what they witnessed and what almost happened.

Kayla raises an eyebrow. "It appears we are in your debt."

"Time enough for that," I say. "Arias is facing off with the Tempest. I need to get back to the shore. You got this?"

She nods. "Yes. Go. And if you have the opportunity, tell my son I was wrong about it. That he can trust you."

We share a look and I nod, then turn and run back to the ocean.

Dead bodies litter the shore, both Fae and bandits, and the bits of the boats the sea creature destroyed float in the surf. Arias has joined the Tempest on the rocks, and they are deep in battle, his sea creature distracted by the black ship cloaked in mist that seems to have a life of its own and looks as if it's somehow fighting the creature.

But still, my money is on the giant serpent that's currently coiling itself around the mid-section of the boat to pull it under water.

The Rider has turned the water around them to ice as their fight gets pushed off the rocks and into the ocean.

I run closer, then tentatively step on the ice. My foot

freezes, so I decide the best course of action is to make a run for it.

So I do.

As I approach the Rider and the Tempest, sword in hand and ready to battle, the Tempest turns to me. Up close, he seems more a mystery than ever. Clothed in black, with a black cape and gold mask that completely covers his face, I can't see any part of skin, hair or eyes. But more than that, the Tempest seems to be cloaked in shadows and darkness, like the mist that surrounds his ship.

Seeing the White Rider in his icy glory against this darkness is an interesting contrast. And I kinda feel like I'm at the world's greatest cosplay contest and I showed up as an old dish rag. So that's super duper.

But I don't need fancy armor or a costume to face my enemies. I'm a badass all my own. So I raise my sword and harden my face. "Show yourself, Tempest. By command of the Hunter's Council."

So, well, I kinda don't want to tell this part. But because we're friends, I will.

The Tempest laughs.

Like, full on belly laugh.

Like I'm a four-year-old with a wooden stick threatening a Class 7 demon kinda laugh.

It's embarrassing. And a bit demoralizing, what with the White Rider standing right here and all.

And then he's has the nerve to say, in his deep rumbly Batman voice, "You think *she* will be able to stop me, Arias? You are a fool. She is but a girl, Unseen Lord or not. She cannot stop what I have come to wrought. I will have that Spirit. You shall see."

So I do what any sane Watcher would do.

I plunge my sword into his chest.

At least, I try to.

But I fail. Because as my steel is about to make contact with his innards, he vanishes in a poof of shadow and darkness.

Just like that.

I look at the Rider, hoping he has an explanation for what just happened, but he's looks as perplexed as me.

As the Tempest's ship sinks to the bottom of the ocean, and the last of his goons are killed, we are left wondering where the hell he went.

"What do we do now?" I ask, dropping my sword onto the ice and shivering. I realize how cold it is, what with the ice and my lack of clothes and all, and the sun is setting. It's been a long day.

And then Arias does something totally unexpected. He pulls off his cloak and places it over my shoulders. "First, we get back to the village, get you cleaned up and clothed, and assess the damage. Then, I show you what we're trying to protect. Assuming my parents don't interfere."

"Oh, we cool," I say. "Your mom cleared me."

He raises an eyebrow at that, but says nothing as we walk together off the ice and away from the ocean. His sea creature shrinks to something very small and rides splinters of ice towards us until he can wrap around the Rider's neck like a choker, and once our feet hit the sand, the ice turns back to waves. It's like the last few hours never happened.

Aside from the dead bodies littering the shore.

ELIAS

$\mathcal{T}$he kingdom spent two days celebrating their new queen. I spent two days organizing our rescue of Iris, as soon as we got a better lead. Aya sent scouts out who knew every inch of Avakiri. If she's on that side of the world, we'll find her.

The lead ends up coming by the most unexpected source.

"Your Highness, there's someone here requesting a personal and private audience with you," one of the servants of High Castle says, standing in the doorway of my quarters.

I've been up for hours, but the sun is still a distant glimmer on the horizon. A fire blazes before me. My bed is a tangled mess of blankets, and I'm wearing nothing but a pair of tie-up leggings. Duke is curled up by the fire sleeping—his favorite place to be.

I sigh. "Who is it?"

The servant, a young Fae who looks to be in her 20s and is unfamiliar to me, curtsies. "She would not give me her name. She is… strange. She says to tell you she helped with your problem in the Black Lotus dungeons and has news for your ears alone."

Callie? It has to be, but how? She disappeared after our escape and no one has heard from her since.

"Send her up," I say, standing to find at least a tunic to throw on. The servant looks nervously at the bed and the clothes on my floor but I wave her away. "My room is fine. Send her up."

A few minutes later, the servant escorts a beautiful woman dressed in a forest green cloak, her head and body covered, and only her face showing. The servant can't stop staring at Callie.

"That will be all. Thank you."

The servant blinks, surprised by my voice, then nervously curtseys and leaves us alone.

Callie takes the chair next to me by the fire and pulls down her hood, revealing small horns and shiny auburn hair. I know underneath her cloak she will also have the furry legs of a succubus.

Callie has been Iris's best friend their whole lives. They were raised together by Sly. Still, I'm surprised to see her here.

Duke wakes from his nap and shuffles over to Callie, laying his head on her lap for a pet, which she naturally obliges.

"You've come a long way," I say.

"You have no idea, Prince. My journeys have taken me far and wide to many of the Nine Worlds."

"And what have you been seeking?"

She looks at me pointedly with piercing chocolate eyes. "Truth."

"That is a hard thing to find," I say. "I've found truth wears many disguises."

She smiles and helps herself to my goblet of wine. "It does indeed. Like a Most Wanted criminal, perhaps."

I learned long ago that succubi have no sway on my

desires. It's rare, but not unheard of for someone to be born immune to their charms. And yet I still find Callie an enjoyable companion, even under these circumstances. "I'm not the truth you're seeking," I say.

"No, you're not. But you are a true thing in a world filled with lies. That's something. And that's what my best friend needs right now."

And so we come to it. "Do you know where she is?"

"I do. And I will tell you, if you promise me something, Prince."

"Anything," I say without hesitation.

She smiles, but there is a sadness to her eyes. "Do not give your promises away so rashly before knowing what I ask."

My jaw hardens. "It doesn't matter what you ask. I will do anything to save Iris."

The fire crackles before us, sending embers sparking into the air, as Callie places a hand on mine. "You two are perfect for each other, if you survive one another that is."

"So tell me. Where is she?"

"First, the promise. When you find her, you must seek the truth, not the easy lie. It won't be easy, but if you are led astray by falsehoods, much will be lost."

"That's fairly ominous," I say with a sigh. Succubi were known to speak in riddles. "Can't you just tell me what to look for."

"I cannot. I would if I could, truly. But I cannot. This is something you must discern for yourself. Keep your eyes open. Trust your heart. You will follow the right path."

Callie stands, giving Duke one last rub, and covers her head again. "When you see my heart-sister, tell her I love her and will be back when I can."

I stand with her and she pulls me into a brief hug, then slips a small bit of parchment into my hand. "Move forward with caution. And remember what I've said."

I nod and watch her leave, wondering how she came into this world and how she will travel from it. Callie always has her ways.

Once alone, I study the paper in my hand. It's coordinates. This must be where Iris is. I can feel it.

I wake Aya and Uncle Asher and we meet in the family quarters, a private part of the castle that's a bit less formal, as far as castles go. It's a large room, but broken into sections for easier conversation, with a huge hearth in the center of the room that's always blazing with a fire. Food and wine have been left on tables and the three of us take chairs near the fire as I share the news of my knowledge, without revealing how I came into it. "I have sources who prefer to remain anonymous," I say.

My uncle accepts that well enough, but Aya looks put out. It doesn't really matter. We know where to go and so we must leave. "How soon can we have the ship ready? Has Uncle Ace finished that contraption of his?"

Aya's eyes light up at that. She loves new gadgets to play with. "Yes! We can leave immediately I would think. I'm certainly done with all the parties and dress-up here."

Uncle Asher clears his throat. "It would not be a good idea for the new queen to leave right now, especially to engage in battle and risk yourself and your brother, the next in line."

She purses her lips. "It's my ship. Of course I'm going. Being queen never stopped my mother from adventuring."

"That was a different time," Asher says. "Things are in turmoil here. Our world needs stability."

She sighs. "My ship has a mirror. I have a mirror. You have a mirror. If anything happens, come get me. Simple. This shouldn't take long. They'll hardly know I've left. And you can manage things well enough without us I would imagine. You've practically been running the kingdom since my parents disappeared, haven't you?"

"That's true enough, but I still feel like this mission is best taken by Elias alone." His tone belied his words, as I could tell he was already caving in to my sister's argument, as everyone is want to do eventually. Once she has something in her mind, you'd be hard pressed to turn her away from it.

She claps her hands and smiles. "Excellent. I'll prepare the ship and my crew. Elias, be ready to go by high noon."

I nod and watch her leave. "The people seem to love her," I say, somewhat wistfully.

Asher turns to me, setting down his goblet of wine. "I'm glad I have a moment alone with you. There's something I've been meaning to tell you."

"What is it?" I ask, curious.

"While it's true, the vote favored your sister from most of the realms," he says slowly.

I nod. "Yes, I figured as much."

"Not all the realms voted for her."

That surprises me. "Really?"

"Your realm voted for you. You are still loved here, despite how it might feel to you. And you are missed. More than I think you know. There is a life waiting for you here if you ever decide to walk a different road."

I'm surprised by how deeply this knowledge affects me, and I blink away the excess emotion building in me. I've always assumed I was hated, especially by my own realm, which I saw as a punishment for not living up to the perfect ideal of a prince. To know that they would have me as their king... it is something significant.

"Perhaps one day, when this mess is over and I'm no longer on the Most Wanted list, there will be a place for me here."

Asher smiles. "That's a start, dear nephew. That's a start."

I take my leave, as there are only a few hours left to pack and prepare. The kitchen is in a flurry, putting together meats, breads, cheeses, fruit and wine for our journey. The servants are helping Aya polish and prep the boat. I excuse my servant to pack for myself. I do not need much.

I look at the coordinates again. We searched a map of Avakiri, but this looks to be in the middle of the ocean. I trust Callie, though. Iris must be there.

At high noon we all gather around Aya's boat, her crew at the ready. I do not like the men she has chosen to follow her. They are hard, cruel and turned by gold more than loyalty, but they are competent and get the job done.

Ace joins us, going over the details of the modifications he made to the Waystone one more time with Aya.

The sun is high in a very blue sky when we set sail. Aya walks the decks barking orders at her crew, though we won't reach any real turbulence until we're off Inferna. These waters are mild and can take a boat through all the seven realms without ever touching land. It's the most efficient way of travel between realms, if you don't have a mirror.

It doesn't take us long to reach the Waystone near Uncle Ace's realm. He has modified it so that the water reaches up to the entrance, giving us easier access on a ship.

Two pillars of stone jut up from the water and Aya maneuvers the ship towards one and presses her hand against it. Blood flows from her palm into the stone, and something below us begins to grind together.

The ship lunges a bit as the water is displaced and a platform rises beneath us, moving us between the pillars. The mechanics of this are incredible, and I wonder how my uncle achieved all this. Normally to use a Waystone we would walk into one after activating it with our blood. This actually took our ship and moved it into place. Remarkable.

Stone walls close around us and the Waystone grinds into motion, taking us deep into the center of our world.

I hear a few of the crew members vomiting, and wonder how they will handle it when the gravity shifts.

Sure enough, mid-way through, everything is turned upside down. I worry the ship will be smashed to bits by this, but large metal stabilizers protrude from the stone to steady the ship and flip it, with us inside, at the exact moment gravity changes.

My stomach drops and I fall to my knees to catch myself. Others do the same. The crew is not happy, by the sounds of it, but Aya ignores them, and so do I.

When we reach Avakiri, we are sent into the world through another bit of engineering magic. The stone rises and lifts the ship into the sea beyond us, then returns to its place, leaving us in the water.

Aya snaps at her crew, getting their attention. "This is the real deal now, boys. Get back to work."

We are truly at sea now, with waves and wind and sun and salt.

There is no visible land in any direction, and I can only trust the navigational skills of my sister to keep us moving in the right direction.

Once we are in a comfortable routine, my sister and I sit on deck with a light dinner and talk.

"Are you enjoying your newfound power?" I ask, already knowing the answer.

"It's temporary," she says. "Mother and Father will return, don't you think?"

"I certainly hope so. I can't bear to imagine what has happened to them."

"What will you do when we find Iris?" she asks.

"What do you mean?"

"Well, she's the Unseen Lord. Her powers could be dangerous. Have you thought about how you'll handle that?"

I bristle at her implication. "She's not mine to handle. I

trust her to use whatever powers she may have for good. She's... she's the best person I've ever known. The purest. She has a code of honor she never breaks. She is guided by a higher moral compass than most. I know she won't do anything that will hurt the innocent."

Aya goes silent after that, and we sit under the stars for a time before she stands, excusing herself. "I need some time alone. See you in the morning?"

I nod and return my gaze to the horizon. My thoughts wander as I contemplate Callie's words of warning. What did she mean? What truth should I be looking for? I don't have any answers, and I worry I will miss the clues when presented to me.

I do not have Iris's moral compass to guide me. Mine broke a long time ago, and I worry I will never get it set right again.

After some time, I retire to my quarters and attempt sleep. It's a restless night of drifting on waves, the rocking of the ship keeping me awake for much of it. Come morning, the day crew is already hard at work, scrubbing the deck, hoisting sails to work with the wind, tracking their progress to stay the course.

I don't see Aya and assume she's either in meetings with her First Mate or taking time alone. She always was a solitary creature growing up, preferring her own company over mine—or her friends—more often than not.

By mid-afternoon there's a buzz in the air, and Aya joins me on deck. She looks tired, but happy. "We should be there soon," she says. "Are you prepared to fight for her?"

"Of course."

It is nearing sunset when the coordinates come into view. It's a remote island, surrounded by mist. That's where the White Rider has been keeping Iris.

My heart beats in my chest and my pulse quickens. We will be together soon.

And if my brother has done anything to harm her... I will destroy him.

IRIS

*A*s we make our way back to the village, I observe the man beside me. This morning I would have called him evil and villainous. Now, as I watch him checking on the wounded we pass and talking with the people—his people—comforting them, encouraging them, I have to wonder about things.

It wasn't so long ago that I would have also called Elias the villain of my story.

These Vane Spero brothers are proving quite the prickly pair for me. Have I really misjudged him so entirely?

"Tell me about this place," I say.

"There are four known tribes of this land, as you are aware."

I nod. "Earth, Air, Fire and Water," I say. This is common knowledge, though I haven't had cause to actually visit any of them, so this is all theoretical to me.

He nods. "There is a fifth that is not known. That is a closely guarded secret. And it lives here on this island."

The little girl I saved earlier runs over to us and throws her arms around me. "You're a god!" she says, her blue eyes wide and adoring. She holds her arms to me and I comply and pick her up to carry her.

"What's your name?" I ask. There wasn't a lot of time for niceties earlier.

"Lala," she says. "Well, that's what mum and pops call me. My real name is big. Want to hear it?"

I nod. "Very much."

"It's Lalunalinkli," she says the syllabus slowly, like they are unfamiliar to her.

"That's an extraordinary name, for an extraordinary girl."

I turn to face the Rider, who has paused to watch us. "Arias, this is Lala. Lala, this is… "

"I know who he is, silly," she says with a giggle. "He's the White Knight who protects us."

"Is he now?" I say, studying the Rider closer. He almost seems to blush at that.

"Where are your parents, little one?" he asks with a softness in his voice I've never heard. "They must be worried."

As if on cue, the mother I met earlier runs over to us. "Lala! I've been looking everywhere for you."

When she realizes who's with her daughter, she nearly gapes. First, she bows to the Rider with tears in her eyes. "Thank you for your protection, my Knight."

Then she hugs me while I'm still holding the kid. "And you, thank you. I can't thank you enough."

"You don't owe us thanks," Arias says. "It is our duty to protect the people of this village."

The mother smiles and nods as I hand Lala over to her.

The little girl smiles and waves as we head to Kayla and Tavian's cottage.

"You saved that family?" he asks.

"I helped out, yes."

"And you found a way to remove your shackles I see," he says, nodding to my hands.

"Remove the hands, remove the shackles."

He shakes his head at that. "You are a strange woman, Watcher. For what it's worth, I'm sorry for what I did to you. I... don't always make the best choices."

He's so awkward I almost feel sorry for him.

"My parents were right about one thing. My plan was foolish and ended badly. I just hope... I hope that even if you can't forgive me, you can at least overlook my own transgressions for the greater good."

We arrive at the cottage, and the night is just starting to give way to the morning as the sun begins its long stretch over the ocean. "I'll listen to what you have to say." It's all I can promise him. But I say it with a heart more open to hearing him now than I had before.

He nods, as if understanding the shift that is happening in me.

Kayla and Tavian aren't home yet, and Arias walks me to a back room that features a large tub filled with hot water. "How did you make this happen?" I ask.

"I have my ways." He provides soaps and salts and oils and dried flowers for my bath, then leaves me to it. "There's a change of clothes for you on the chair there. Help yourself. I'll be in the living room ready to explain everything when you're done."

I would be lying if I said the bath wasn't the most luxurious experience of my life. Hot soapy scented water helps slough off the shit and grime in my skin and hair, and when I'm done, I am shiny and pink and smell like a rose.

The clothes he provided are better than I expect. Undergarments, white pants that fit loosely and are made out of a super comfy light, soft fabric, plus a belted tunic in the same color and fabric and soft leather sandals. It's an outfit very much in the style of the people here, and I finally feel like I fit in a little better.

When I return to the living room, Arias is waiting for me with a plate of hot food and a mug of wine. I drink and eat while I wait for him to explain.

"There's an ancient power on this island that we've been protecting for generations. It is the Storm Spirit, the fifth elemental of the Druids."

I stop eating. "There's another Druid?"

"No, just another Spirit," his eyes focusing on the past. "Long ago, in the early days of Avakiri, before the vampires were cast to this world, a prince coveted the power of the Midnight Star and killed his mother to get it for himself. But the Spirit chose his sister, and she was whisked away to protect her from her brother's jealously and wrath. Before they could capture the prince, he discovered a way of creating a fifth Spirit: that of the Storm, and with that became the fifth Druid. His powers were greater than any of the other Spirits, and rather than him controlling his Spirit, it controlled him. It turned him truly evil, beyond anything he'd been before. Now he wanted to destroy all the worlds, not just rule his own. The Midnight Star died to stop her brother from complete destruction, but she had recently given birth to a baby boy who the Midnight Star passed to. She stopped her brother by capturing his Spirit and imprisoning it. Here. She had help from the other Druids, of course, but it was her sacrifice that made it possible. Since then, this island, these people, have been kept a secret, even from the other Fae. The families who live here have been raised here for generations. But now the Tempest knows where the Spirit is. We aren't safe. We must destroy him before he gets the Spirit. He could end all the worlds with the power of the Storm."

Well, crap. "Can't you destroy it?" I ask.

"Many have tried. The best we can do is contain it."

"So no one who is born here ever leaves?" I ask. I mean,

it's a lovely place. A paradise, even. But I'd be hard-pressed to stay in one place that long.

"There are a few over the many years who have asked to leave. We have a process for them. They must give up their memories of this place and all who live here. They can never return. That is the price they must pay to leave."

I take a big drink of my wine and another bite of a chicken leg before replying. "That's a steep price. And people are willing to do that?"

He nods. "Some. Not many, but every generation a few will choose to."

"And what about criminals?" I ask. "What's your law and order like here?"

"My parents keep the peace mostly. It's a small community so we don't have big crimes. But in the past, if there's a murder done in cold blood, or a rape or other violent crime, that person is forcibly stripped of their memories and Tavian takes them to Inferna for punishment."

"Do you spend a lot of time here?" I ask.

"I did," he says. "When I was a child. I grew up here. Then I left when I thought my presence was a danger to my parents and those I loved. I came back as an adult, but I had changed. They had changed. The world, it seemed, had changed."

I have nothing to say to that, so I eat quietly for a time. When I'm finished, I ask if there's more food.

"Are you still hungry, even after all that?" he asks.

"No, but I know someone who is. Also, can you have a bath sent to the cave your mother is in, a table, chairs, food, a comfortable bed and a change of clothes. The queen deserves better than what she has. I understand she has to stay in the cave while she's under a spell, but she doesn't have to suffer unnecessarily," I say.

The Rider bows his head. "You are right. I will have those things done at once."

I clean up the kitchen and wash our dishes while he makes arrangements with Kayla and Tavian, the only other two who know she's here. Between the four of us, we manage to bring everything to the cave that I've asked for.

Tavian and Kayla leave to help rebuild huts that were destroyed during the fighting, and help heal and care for those who are wounded. I'm guessing Kayla will be making more of her disgusting but effective cure-all.

Arias looks at me helplessly. "Be careful. There's a reason we haven't done more for her. She's dangerous and unstable. None of us can be in there long without it turning bad quickly."

"I got this," I say. "I'm not chained anymore, and my Renewal is back up should things turn seriously shitty."

He nods and leaves me alone with the broken woman lying in the dirt.

"Arianna?" I whisper so as not to alert her. "Hey. How about we get you cleaned up and get some food in you."

I approach her cautiously and help her stand. She's like a rag doll in my arms, but she doesn't crumble to the ground when I release her, so that's progress. She can't stand up straight with her chains, but I extend them as far as I can. "I'm going to help you undress, okay?"

She gives a single nod, and I take that as consent and peel away the torn, stained gown she's wearing. Standing there naked, it's clear she's undernourished.

First, though, I need to get her clean. I guide her to the bath and help her in, then use a sponge to scrub her skin and hair clean.

She's silent through it all.

The bath water is black when she emerges, but she is back to her pale self with long dark hair. I dry her briskly with a towel, then help her dress and lead her over to the table where food awaits.

"You need to eat, okay?"

She gives another nod and nibbles at a berry.

Despite all my care, she still looks like a hollowed out person. I had hoped this would help. Maybe she'll at least be more comfortable.

I sigh and move to stand, but she grabs my wrist with a force I wasn't expecting.

"The prophecy foretold this," she says in a haunting voice.

"What prophecy? What do you mean?" I try to pry my wrist out of her grip, but the woman is latched on tight.

Her eyes kinda freak me out, rolling around like she's following the light of some psychedelic optometrist. "It was foretold, but wasn't understood. Great crimes were committed. Now, it shall come to pass. My blood. My blood. My blood is bad."

She releases me and curls into a ball, pulling her legs onto her chair and rocking back and forth, her hair, still wet, falling over her face. I'll be honest here, she looks a bit like the creepy girl from that one horror movie. With all the hairs? Like, am I gonna be haunted in seven days or something?

She continues rocking and moaning about her blood being bad, and I don't know what to do. "I'm sorry, Arianna. I'm so sorry this is happening to you."

I leave the cave, hoping my ministrations have helped at least a little, and find Arias using his Druid powers to create a small pool of water for a few kids to play in. He compels the water to form the shapes of mermaids, dolphins and birds and laughs as the children splash and attempt to catch the creatures. I hate to interrupt him, but I have questions. So. Many. Questions.

Arias says goodbye to the children when he sees me, and strides over. "How is the queen?"

"Not herself," I say. "But I have a question for you. She told me you captured her by baiting her with news about her son. Why?"

He frowns and purses his lips. "Is that what she said? Hm. No, that's not what happened. Truth is, she found me and attacked me in the middle of the night. She didn't have Yami, her dragon, with her, or I would likely be dead right now. She was out of her mind with madness, so I had to subdue her. I took her here to be examined by Kayla, which is when we realized she'd been cursed by the Tempest."

"How did you figure out the Tempest did it?"

"Things she said. But also, Tavian used magic to probe her and recognized the strands of power left behind."

"So where's Fen? When Elias and I were traveling in Inferna, we found a wolf pup that was Baron's offspring. Baron died, but will be reborn. But Fen wasn't with him. And where's her dragon?"

"I don't have these answers, Watcher. I wish I did."

Well, that's less than helpful.

As I consider my next question, because man-oh-man do I have a bunch, a fat drop of water lands on my face. Then another. And another, until a deluge of rain breaks from the sky, drenching us in a matter of seconds.

Arias stares at the drops on his hand, perplexed.

I chuckle. "What, never seen rain before?"

Thunder shakes the earth—like literally—as lightning cracks through the sky. Okay, this is a bit more than rain, I suppose.

"This isn't right. I have to go." He takes off in a sprint towards the shore, and of course I follow him because what else am I gonna do? You know me, little bird. I need to be where the action is.

When we reach the shore, the sky is heavy with dark clouds, and the early evening twilight is lit up by lightning.

But the storm seems to be generating not from above, but from the rocks where Arias and the Tempest fought.

Arias raises his arms and parts the waters that separate us from the rocks.

"Neat trick," I say.

He doesn't respond, but doesn't tell me not to come as he walks along the bottom of the ocean floor to reach the rocks. Not that I would have gone back had he told me to. I don't really do well following orders.

It's a longer walk than I expected, and I'm careful not to step on small displaced sea creatures who are wondering where the hell all the water went.

When we arrive, I see a hidden cave entrance that wouldn't be visible if Arias hadn't parted the sea like a modern-day Moses. "Be very careful when we descend," he says. "And do not attempt to connect with any powers you might sense within."

I'm intrigued and I'm guessing we're about to come face to face with whatever this Storm Spirit is. I follow him into the cave, the hair on my arms rising in salute of whatever powers pulse around me.

A surge of electric force dances on my skin as we descend deeper into the darkness, causing me to stumble into the Rider, who catches me and helps me stand upright. Just as I'm about to ask for some kind of illumination—since this pitch black isn't exactly a walk in the park—small bursts of light begin to flash around us.

Like little shots of lightning, trapped underground.

The air stirs as we move deeper towards the Storm Spirit.

The magic trapped down here is big. Powerful. And entirely unstable.

I can feel it testing me, pushing against me. Looking for an opening.

Looking for a way in.

My eyes widen and I reach for the Rider's arm. "Stop," I say.

He stops. Listens. His eyes widen. "What did you do?" he asks.

"I've done nothing." But something is happening. The space around us is filling with electric jolts of lightning energy, like our very own personal storm. The rock we are encased in begins to rumble, cracking, crumbling, as the power grows.

"It's breaking free of its containment," Arias says, and it's the first time I've ever heard fear in his voice. It does not bring me comfort. "We need to leave."

"Ya think?" In retrospect, I should have let him come to this alone.

He turns to guide us out, but it's too late.

We've waltzed into the bowels of the earth.

We are now under the ocean. I can practically feel the weight of the water pressing in around us. The way all sound is dimmed.

My skin begins to itch.

My mind begins to crawl with memories best left in the past.

The walls around me begin to close in, stifling my breath.

Smothering my lungs.

Lightning blasts at the stone around us, tumbling bits of rock and earth, causing the cave to collapse, with us in it.

We are both thrown to the ground, covered in dirt and rock as it pours over us like water until we can't breathe.

I'm only scared of three things.

Spiders is one of them.

And being buried alive is another.

IRIS: A SHORT STORY INTERLUDE

*J*n the time before, during that in-between stage of childhood and adulthood, I endured the second great trauma of my life.

Being a teenager is hard enough under any circumstance. Being a teenager raised by Uncle Sly in the Black Lotus and homeschooled, as it were, with classes like "The Myths and Histories of the Nine Worlds," and "Survival 101: Were-wolves, Witches and Wargs," made my teenage life particularly challenging.

I knew how to kill a man—or beast—twelve different ways by my thirteenth birthday, only three of those requiring weapons. By my sixteenth birthday I could identify the top five herbs most useful for poisoning and tell you which were best for fast results, and which were preferred for slow and painful deaths. I'd mastered over a dozen different weapons, settling on my dual wielding daggers as my personal favorites. And I was well on my way to mastering the intricacies of the Hunter's Code. I was determined to be the best Hunter of all time, and the youngest Watcher the Council had ever seen.

You can see how I didn't change much through the years.

What I hadn't mastered at that point was the subtle nuances of what would become the most treacherous foe I would face as a girl... boys.

I was the worst at flirting. I could kick their asses. Kill them even (though that was generally frowned upon). But woo them? Entice them into a relationship? Nope. Nada. Ain't happening.

You'd think having a succubus as a bestie/sister would give me an advantage. After all, the two of us were inseparable, and we were always trailed by a gaggle of boys looking to gain Callie's attention. You'd think her charm and charisma would rub off on me, right?

Yeah, it didn't. If anything, it had the opposite effect. She shone so brightly that not only did I live in her shadow, but what was, in retrospect, totally normal teenager awkwardness was so much more glaring in comparison to her otherworldliness.

I never resented her. Not at all. Instead, I threw myself into being the most badass Hunter-in-Training the Council had ever seen.

I lived and breathed everything related to being a Hunter. I would have made Buffy the Vampire Slayer look like an amateur.

And I was content with that. I didn't need the distraction of a guy anyways. I had Uncle Sly and Callie and my tutors and all the strange and magnificent beings who came to the Black Lotus and took turns teaching me their skills and telling me stories of their worlds. Who needed teenage boys when you had all that?

And this worked. I was happy.

Until I met Him, with a capital H.

That's when it all came crashing down. The unshakable,

unwavering confidence I had built into my life. My discipline and dedication to my training. All of it.

It was the summer just after I turned 16. So cliche, I know. The summer the Council held a summit at the Black Lotus and invited royal convoys from several of the Nine Worlds.

He was from Nirandel, the world of dragons, and he was a Twin Spirit, meaning he carried with him a companion spirit that he could summon. A raven, black as night. He had hair the color of his bird, and eyes that matched, with skin so pale he could have passed as a vampire. He was with the convoy from Dragoncliff Academy, a training school on Nirandel for Twin Spirits. The Black Lotus was packed with beings of all kinds. There wasn't a room to spare. Even Jesus would have been sent to the barn that summer. And they would all be staying for three glorious months. But Devon was the only one I had eyes for.

Uncle Sly had costume balls and extravagant galas planned in between late night meetings that only the highest dignitaries were invited to. It was a peace conference of sorts. A chance for different sects of the magical community on different worlds to air their grievances and find common ground.

I wanted desperately to attend the meetings. At least, I did before Devon showed up and I realized he wouldn't be in them either.

The other thing I realized pretty quickly was he didn't light up whenever Callie walked into the room. He didn't follow her around like a lost puppy. He didn't drool at every word she spoke.

But he did find opportunities to talk to me. To ask me about the Black Lotus. About Uncle Sly's extensive library. About my favorite books. About myself and what it was like to live here.

It started the first night everyone arrived. Uncle Sly planned a casual dinner—well as casual as my uncle ever gets... no jeans or sweats in sight—followed by live entertainment and free flowing liquor for the adults, provided by the Nelpam Tribes. They were known for their powerful spirits—and I don't mean actual spirits, though you might think you see them after drinking their liquor, I've heard. I've never tested this myself of course.

Which is how Devon and I met.

I snuck a bottle of Firebolt from the festivities and left for my secret spot in which to hide and imbibe in the forbidden. Winding through the long stone hallways draped in ancient tapestries, I slipped through a door masquerading as a painting and onto a private balcony overlooking a secret garden that only Uncle Sly and I knew about. I hadn't even told Callie about this place, for I wanted one spot that was mine alone. Only when I arrived, bottle of liquor in hand, it was already taken. A boy was there, sitting on my bench—a bench Uncle Sly had commissioned for me as a surprise, though he himself never came to this balcony. We had a silent agreement that he always respected. The boy had a book opened on his lap and seemed engrossed in it. Candles floated in the air, illuminating the space with dancing flickers of firelight.

I jolted back in shock upon finding him, and he closed his book and looked at me, then smiled.

"What are you doing here?" I asked, indignant.

"I'm sorry, am I intruding? I needed a quiet spot away from all those people, and this seemed to call out to me through the walls." He raised his hand and his skin glowed an iridescent white. "It's one of my gifts."

"Oh. Um. No, it's okay I guess. Just... don't tell anyone about this place. It's mine." I flinched at how childish I sounded, but I couldn't help it. I didn't want a bunch of strangers traipsing all over my special spot. It would defile it.

"You're Iris," he said, without a question mark.

"Yes. How…?"

He shrugged, slipping his book into a hidden pocket of his black cloaks. "Everyone knows the niece of Sly the Mysterious. You're quite an enigma."

I raised an eyebrow at that. I'd never been called an enigma before and found I quite liked it. "I don't know about that. I just… keep to myself mostly."

He grinned at me, revealing a dimpled left cheek that did strange things to my stomach. "That's what makes you an enigma. Your friend, she's out there, center of attention. Anyone can get to know her. But you… you're like a shadow. A mystery. An intrigue."

My face flushed hot at his unexpected compliments. To distract myself from this new and slightly uncomfortable feeling, I held up the bottle I'd swiped. "Want to try it?"

The boy nodded and held out his hand. "I'm Devon by the way. From Dragoncliff."

"Nice to meet you," I said, in my most grown up manner, then sat next to him on the bench facing the garden below. This was a special place, not just because of how private it was, but because of the garden itself. It contained rare plants found on other worlds, gifts given to Uncle Sly over the centuries. He cultivated them and created a magical world in the little space. At night it was particularly magnificent, as many of the flowers and plant glowed in the darkness, casting rays of color into the night. Light bugs floated lazily around a flower the size of man. It only bloomed at night under a full moon, and we happened to catch it at just the right time.

"This is an incredible place," Devon said.

I nodded and studied the liquor. The bottle was clear,

showcasing a fire red liquid. The glass was said to be made from the sand dunes of Elythia, but those are unsubstanti-ated rumors since that land is uninhabitable. I ran a finger over the etchings on the bottle, hieroglyphs in the style of the Nelpam Tribe. I could only make out a few words. Language wasn't my strongest class, and there were so many to learn. Uncle Sly wanted me at least passingly familiar with all of them.

As I pulled the cork off, the smell hit me hard and fast and, had I been alone, I likely would not have touched it. But Devon looked at me expectantly, so I couldn't chicken out.

I took a swig and felt an instant burn in my mouth that trailed all the way down my throat and into my gut. I was pretty sure this vile liquid could burn the scales off a dragon, but I grimaced without sound and passed it to Devon, watching his reaction carefully.

He took a generous gulp, but his face held steady, as if he was drinking a lemon mint spritzer and not the acidic discharge from a demon's hindquarters.

When he handed the bottle back to me, my eyes widened in reflexive fear. I could already feel the effects of this magical concoction and worried for what it would do to me if I continued to consume it.

He looked at me expectantly, his dark eyes drilling into mine. I smiled like this was something I did all the time—it wasn't—and took another gulp, the smallest one I could without looking like a wuss.

His eyebrow raised, as if impressed, then he doubled the amount he took in. This time, he couldn't hide the effects. His face turned red and eyes bugged out as he tried not to choke. I took the bottle from him as he held in a cough. I was on the verge of laughter but tried to suppress it. Laughing at him seemed a bad idea, but then he started laughing, and it broke the tension between.

I set the bottle down, gently plugging it back up with the cork, and we laughed longer than the experience required. The heat that burned into me now spread throughout my body and everything felt lighter. The glowing flowers of the garden danced in a wind I could see but not feel, as everything around me moved and swayed.

Or maybe it was just me moving and swaying. I couldn't tell anymore.

"Is this your first time drinking?" he asked, after a long moment of silence.

Had I been sober, I would have lied, but it seemed the liquor stripped me of my inhibitions—and my ability to bluster. "Yes."

I leaned back against the stone wall behind us, my body limp and loose. "You probably do this all the time," I said.

He laughed at that. "What makes you think so?"

I shrugged. "Don't know. You seem the type."

"And what type is that?"

"Brooding, rebellious. Not held back by rules." The things I secretly wanted to be but never had to the guts to really do. Truth be told, this was the first time I'd really—for real—broken the rules Uncle Sly had for me. And honestly, it wasn't a biggie. I hated to admit it about myself, but I was a rule follower, through and through.

It was something I was working on. Maybe being around Devon would be good for me. He could help me cultivate a more rebel image.

"Interesting," he said, but offered nothing more about whether my assessment of him was correct or not. "Tell me about you, Iris. What makes you tick?"

"Um…" I didn't think he wanted to hear about my training. Besides, I'd heard stories about the training kids received at Dragoncliff Academy. He'd probably scoff at what I did. "There's not much to tell really. I've been raised here all my life. I'll eventually become a Hunter, once I'm old enough. Shouldn't be too long now." Uncle Sly had promised I could take the Hunter test soon, and though he'd never quite defined what 'soon' meant, I was going to hold him to my definition of the word.

Devon nodded somberly. "Want to see something?" he asked.

"Sure."

He held out his hand and a flurry of light flickered over it until a beautiful black raven appeared, perching serenely. "This is Pitch. He's my Spirit. You can pet him if you want."

I'd never been this close to a raven before, or any bird really. I ran a finger down the soft feathers and the bird closed his eyes as if he enjoyed it.

"I have two llamas," I said. "But I can't summon them."

"I've never met a llama before," he said.

"I can introduce you tomorrow after breakfast if you want."

He smiled. "That would be nice."

* * *

AND SO THE SUMMER WENT. Devon and I were inseparable. For weeks we ate together, explored the grounds together. I showed him secret passages and introduced him to our regulars. It would have been the perfect summer if not for one thing.

That was the summer Callie and I had the worst fight of our friendship. And it was because of Devon.

"I'm happy for you, Iris, I really am," she said, her cute little horns polished and glittering in the lights of the crystal chandeliers suspended above us. "Just… be careful. You don't know him. Not really. And it's just gotten… really intense, really fast."

Tears burned my eyes and my temper flared to cover the pain in my heart. "You just can't stand that a boy likes me and not you for the first time ever. Why can't you just let me have this one thing?"

She jerked back as if I'd slapped her. "I can't believe you would think that of me. I want you to be happy, I just think you're going too fast."

"You're just a selfish bitch who needs the attention of everyone all the time!" I screamed at her, spittle flying from my mouth.

Her lips puckered and face hardened, but she held her tongue, turning on her heels to walk away. We didn't speak for the next several weeks.

Which seriously sucked, because she's the one person I needed to talk to when Devon and I kissed for the first time.

It was magical. In our secret garden under a crescent moon. He held my face in his hand, caressing my cheek. "You're the most beautiful girl I've ever known," he said, before bringing his face down until our lips touched. It was a soft kiss, gentle and timid at first, and my body was lit on fire by the contact. I'd kissed a boy before, when I was fourteen. He was a Fae visiting with his family and it was a peck on the lips while we were in the barn with the llamas. It was my first kiss. His too, I think.

But it was nothing like this.

As the kiss deepened into something more than a kiss, I pressed my body closer to Devon and his arm slipped around my waist, pulling me closer still. My arms drifted to his shoulders, my fingers twining into his messy dark hair.

When he pulled away, I felt breathless and weak-kneed. It was incredible.

"I wish you didn't have to go at the end of the summer," I said after, as we walked hand in hand through the garden.

"I would stay forever if I could."

Keeping in touch through different worlds is tricky. There are ways. Uncle Sly has a system, and I vowed I would write letters. They would take forever to get there, but it was something.

As the summer drew to a close, and our days and nights together became numbered, he led me to his guest room. The bed was covered in rose petals and a fire blazed to cut the cold.

We had done everything but the actual deed of sex, and I was ready. I was ready to lose myself in the ultimate bliss.

He was gentle. Tender. Loving. It hurt only a moment, and then it felt right. Perfect.

After, he held me and we kissed and talked and I didn't think life could get more perfect than it was in that moment.

"You are still my personal enigma," he said that night, brushing a dark lock of hair off my forehead.

I didn't know what to say to that, so I just smiled and laid my head on his chest. I could hear his heartbeat. Thump thump. Thump thump. I wanted to stay this way forever.

"You and Sly seem very close," he said after a time.

It was an odd moment to bring up my uncle, but he wasn't wrong. "Yes. Very."

"He must tell you things he doesn't tell anyone else."

I shrugged. "I guess so."

"Do you think...? No, never mind. Sorry. I'm being stupid."

I propped myself up and faced him. "What?"

"Well, it's just that, I heard stories about a secret vault under the Black Lotus that holds treasure. I don't care about the treasure, but they say it also holds a staff that was used by an ancient and powerful sorcerer. If the stories are true, that might have belonged to my family, and... I've always wanted to see it. To hold it. I have no family left, and I feel like being able to touch the staff would connect me to my family again."

His story broke my heart, and I agreed to help him find this secret vault. I didn't precisely know where it was, but I knew where to start looking.

In the dungeons.

That night while the Council meetings were taking place with the top dignitaries, we snuck into the hidden passages in the walls, winding through cobwebs and dusty pathways until we reached the bowels of the dungeons.

The smell of sulfur, blood, piss and excrement assaulted us the moment we stepped into the dark, dank place.

"If there's an entrance it would be here," I said, pulling him along by the hand.

He wrinkled his nose in disgust. "Do you spend a lot of time down here?"

I scoffed at that. "Nope. But it was part of my training. I was locked in a cell and had to try to escape."

He snorted. "How'd that end?"

"Not well. This place is inescapable. It's why Uncle Sly is entrusted with the worst magical criminals. Because everyone knows once they're here, they won't escape."

I tried not to make eye contact with the few prisoners we passed, and I avoided the guards at all cost. They liked me well enough, but 1: they would totally rat me out to Uncle Sly that I was nosing around down here and 2: they made a living torturing people. So they weren't on my top list of favs. Truth be told, they made my skin crawl.

We turned a corner and at the sound of a guard approaching I pulled Devon into an empty cell and closed it softly, putting a finger over his lips so he'd stay quiet as the guard passed.

It was a burly demon, red-skinned, and dragging a bloody morning star—a club-like weapon with a ball of spikes attached to a shaft.

Devon sucked in his breath, but didn't speak until the

guard passed us. Even still, I cautioned silence until I could no longer hear the metal dragging against the stone floor.

"That was... intense... " Devon said.

I nodded and led him deeper into the darkness.

I'd heard whispers from the guards of things hidden beneath the dungeons, but I'd never ventured forth to explore. Hadn't felt the need to, until then.

The dungeons gave me the creeps.

The smell made me nauseous.

But when I saw the excitement in Devon's eyes as he anticipated holding his family's staff again, I pushed forward, knowing it would be worth it.

I've always had a connection to the Black Lotus that went beyond my years of living there. It wasn't just a building to me, but a being that I'd bonded with.

I used that bond to feel into the bones of the place, letting my mind penetrate the deeper layers as we explored the lesser used parts of the dungeons.

"The cells here are the original ones used when the Black Lotus was first formed a thousand years ago. New, magically reinforced cells utilizing trimantium were later built, and these became relics of another time," I explained in my best history professor voice as we cautiously made our way through. If there was a secret door anywhere it would in the most ancient part of the dungeon. "Now my uncle uses this section for storage, mostly," I said, gesturing to a cell that was packed with dusty boxes and furniture covered in plastic. "He's a bit of a pack rat."

"Fascinating," Devon said, without a trace of sarcasm.

"There's a cell back here that he never stores stuff in," I said. "I asked him about it once and he just shrugged but didn't answer. I'm thinking we might find something there."

We reached the cell in question, and I pulled out my master key and unlocked it, opening the steel bars and stepping in. Devon follows me, and I look around the small, boxed space, hoping for some kind of clue.

The floor was dirt-covered stone. The walls were steel bars. That was about it. Nothing else. I jammed the tips of my boots into the the ground, kicking up dust. As I continued kicking at the ground, I listened carefully for any changes. "There!" I said, stopping. "This spot is different than the rest. Help me."

I dropped to my knees and used my hands to brush dirt away. Devon looked at me skeptically but helped. We didn't make a lot of progress initially, and both our hands were getting raw and sore, but just as Devon was ready to give up, a glint of metal caught my eye. "Something's there!"

We renewed our efforts and after what felt like forever, our hard work paid off. I sat on my knees, exhausted and covered in dirt. We had found a secret door leading somewhere beneath the dungeons. It was locked, and so I tried my key, mostly expecting it to fail. But to my surprise, we heard a click and a shift of metal. "Holy hell balls, I think it worked."

Devon leaned over and pulled on the latch, disrupting the dirt stuck in cracks and crevices that hands alone couldn't remove. It clearly hadn't been opened in who knows how many years, and yet the metal was rust free. Magic had its uses.

A ladder descended from the door's edge into a dark abyss. Devon held up his hand and manifested a ball of white light.

"Neat trick," I said, impressed.

He shrugged. "Everyone at my school can do stuff like this. I'm not that special."

There was a bitterness in his voice I hadn't noticed before, but I shrugged it off. Who didn't feel a twinge of insecurity now and then? Especially at our age.

"Well, I think it's pretty cool. I don't have any fun magical abilities," I said, letting my own resentment leak through my words.

Devon smiled at me, his dimple melting my insides. "You don't need them. You *are* the magic."

No one had ever spoken to me like that, and it filled me with a special kind of pride and glow that I'd never had before.

"Ladies first?" he said, gesturing to the darkness.

"Age before beauty," I teased, trying not to let my nerves show.

There was a reason Uncle Sly kept this hidden. A reason it wasn't part of my training.

A twinge of uncertainty ran up my spine, and I shivered. My gut said to turn and go, but I couldn't disappoint Devon.

With a sigh I didn't let escape my lips, I led the way, taking tentative steps down the ladder. Devon's ball of light stayed with us, but the darkness was so thick, almost soup-like, that the magical rays only illuminated a small sphere around us. So I could only see a few steps below me.

I fought off visions of monsters leaping from the depths of the dark to grab my feet with sharp teeth and pull me into hell. My heart pounded and sweat beaded on my skin. I breathed through it. I was training to be a Hunter. I would need to face much scarier situations than this. I'd already faced scarier situations, I reminded myself, thinking of the girl I thought a friend, who nearly killed me in the end. I shivered and hoped there wouldn't be any spiders down here. They were the only things I was truly scared of. Uncle Sly said I needed to face my fears, work through them. I told him it was a fear because I *had* faced them. I don't need a rehash of that traumatic moment, thank you very kindly.

"Can you see anything?" Devon asked in a whisper that seemed to die on his lips. It's as if the air around us swallowed all sound along with the light. It was a hungry darkness, consuming everything in its wake. Would it consume us as well?

"Nothing yet," I said, pushing a false bravery into my voice that I so did not feel. Hey, fake it till you make it, right?

He didn't say anything after that, and we kept climbing down.

My arms shook and my hands became slick with sweat, making my grip on the rope ladder tenuous at best. I wasn't tired, per se. I trained hard physically and had done much more demanding labors than this. But the adrenaline, nerves, fear and anticipation were building in me and creating an unstable cocktail in my body. I didn't like the feeling.

In the oppressive silence Devon's breath seemed muted, but mine practically screamed in my own head, filling me with a dread I couldn't easily define. The end of the ladder arrived before any definable landing spot did, and I hung there, unsteady, unsure what to do next.

"Why'd you stop?" Devon asked.

"There's no more ladder," I said, trying to keep my voice calm.

"Then drop the rest of the way," he said.

"Are you mad? I can't even see the bottom. Best case scenario I break my leg. Worst case, I die and my body rots here for all eternity."

"I'm sure it will be fine. Why would your uncle have a way into this place if it wasn't effective?"

My voice became pinched in irritation. "Maybe he hasn't been down here in ages and doesn't realize the ladder broke. Maybe he has another way in and this way is for fools who flirt with an early death. It was a bit too easy to break into, don't you think?"

"Not really," Devon said. "You have that key. How many other people have a key like that?"

"No one," I admitted. "I mean, Uncle Sly has a Skeleton

Key to everything, but this key has other special abilities." I'd already said too much about something that was supposed to be a secret. Or at least treated with a certain level of caution. I clamped my mouth shut, irritated at myself for confiding so much.

Devon sighed. "Maybe I can help." He paused, going still. I watched him from below, not catching a lot of what he was doing, but I did see when Pitch, his black raven, appeared before him. "Pitch, fly down there and scope it out for us, will you?"

Pitch, seeming to understand him, flew past me in a whoosh. He flapped his wings hard, apparently affected by the heaviness of this dark air, just as we were.

It only took a moment for Pitch to let out a caw that sounded reasonably close.

"See?" Devon said. "The floor is right there. We just can't see it. Drop. I'll be right behind you."

Everything in me said this was a bad idea, but in for a penny, in for a pound, as they say. I didn't actually know who said that or what it meant. Seemed to me if you lost a penny being stupid, you wouldn't want to add a pound to that mistake. But whatever. I was about to throw all my valuables into my mistake.

Those valuables being my bones and internal organs, naturally.

I readied myself, relaxing my muscles and preparing for a combat landing as I'd been taught.

And then, I released my hands and dropped.

Fear swelled up in my chest and I fought the instinct to contract my muscles and stiffen. That would make the impact more painful and dangerous, however far down it was. Instead, I made myself relax. I would roll into the landing, easing my body into it.

Not knowing when I would hit the floor was the hardest

part.

I couldn't anticipate until it was already happening.

But instinct and years of training kicked in and I nailed the landing like a pro.

The ball of light had stayed with Devon, so I couldn't see my hand in front of me, let alone what else might be around. I shivered and raised my voice. "All clear. Come on down."

I stepped back so he wouldn't land on me, and hoped I wouldn't walk into something super creepy.

Skeletons would be okay.

As long as they were still dead.

But really, I preferred nothing dead or living.

Devon dropped gracefully in front of me. I could hear him more than see him. But the ball of light joined us and gave some illumination to the depths of the darkness.

"We made it," he said.

"Mmhmm." Like an idiot, I only just then considered how we were going to get out of there. It wasn't too long of a drop. I might be able to jump.

I shrugged. One problem at a time.

"Let's find your family's staff," I said with more enthusiasm than I felt.

Devon sent the light orbiting around us, and as my vision focused, I sucked in a breath. We stood in the middle of more treasure than I'd ever imagined in my life. Gold, jewels, chests overflowing with priceless heirlooms. It was a stunning display of wealth. A pirate's wet dream, to be sure.

Devon seemed unimpressed though. "I don't see the staff," he said, his voice thick with disappointment.

"We've only just begun looking," I said, surprised at his surliness. "Let's keep looking."

It took several hours. That's how big the cavern was. And it wasn't with the main treasure. We finally found it deep inside the underground caverns in its own dank little carved out hole, propped against the dirt wall.

Given its surroundings, it looked unremarkable at best. A wooden staff, simply made, carved inexpertly, with a crystal atop it.

But Devon acted as though his every wish and dream had come true. His eyes widened, and lips parted, and he practically glowed with anticipation.

I reached toward the staff, prepared to pass it to him, but his voice stopped me.

"Don't touch it!" He barked, his voice hard and angry.

I flinched and pulled back, surprised at his tone.

He softened his face at my reaction. "Sorry, it's just—no one has touched it for many years and I kinda wanted to be the first. You know? Since it was my family's?"

His explanation sounded reasonable, but something felt off in my gut. Still, I trusted him, so I stood back and let him walk forward.

He had the eyes of a fanatic as he gripped the piece of wood in his hand.

The touch sent a spark of something electric into his eyes and he smiled.

His raven, Pitch, appeared before him, and Devon spoke to his bird. "It's time. Are you ready?"

The raven landed on the crystal ball atop the staff and Devon closed his eyes.

At that moment, everything changed.

Shards of lightning exploded from the crystal, striking every surface around us. I screamed and dropped to the ground to make a smaller target as I considered how to save Devon, but when I looked, I realized he didn't need saving.

I could see by his face, this was exactly what he wanted to happen.

His eyes glowed white, and flashes of electricity burned

in his pupils and under his skin, like he'd been plugged in to a storm.

His bird turned from black to white, and discharged lightning as it flew around the small space.

"What are you doing?" I screamed.

"I'm claiming what's rightfully mine! Now the Council will bow to me. Nirandel will bow to me. The Nine Worlds will bow to me!"

Oh shit. This was definitely not how I imagined this going.

With those words, my eyes opened. Like the blind gaining vision, I suddenly saw all that I had ignored before. All the warning signs.

The questions about the Black Lotus and Uncle Sly. The long tours into secret tunnels. The rapt attention at anything related to the mysteries of the place I'd grown up.

He wasn't courting me, he was using me to scout for him. And I was too blind to see it.

Callie had been trying to warn me, without hurting my feelings, and I had treated her like dirt.

I was the worst friend. And the stupidest girl to ever walk any of the worlds.

I had been duped by a pretty face and sweet words.

But I could kick myself later. Right now, I had bigger problems to deal with.

Like the fact that my boyfriend was going supernova on me. What the fu—?

The earth around us and above us shook and chunks of dirt and rock began to break away as zaps of lightning tore at the walls and ceiling. A ceiling which was actually the floor of the dungeons.

This was bad.

Really bad.

"What are you doing?" I screamed again, somehow hoping his answer would change. "What is that thing really?"

His eyes shone with such intensity I couldn't look straight at him. The silver thunderbolts crawled under his skin, growing brighter, or maybe his skin was thinning. It was hard to tell.

"This is what I was destined to become," he said, his voice no longer that of the boy I thought I was falling in love with. It was filled with something else now. A darker power that stripped out anything human.

"You were already powerful," I said. "You already had so much. Why do this?"

Fear gripped me. I knew I had to stop him before he left this place. I knew I had to end this now. Here. Or too many others would be at risk. I didn't understand the power he held or what he could do, but I knew it wouldn't end well if he was let loose on the worlds.

I stepped closer to him, clenching my fists, wishing I had my twin daggers with me. But I didn't think I needed my weapons. Not here. Not with him.

Keep him talking. I needed to keep him talking.

"Explain this to me. I want to understand."

"This is the power of the gods," he said. "And now it is mine. It was stolen from my ancestors and our power was stripped from us. It was my destiny to get it back. To fulfill my duty to lead."

"What power is this?" I had to scream now. The staff was generating a storm, with winds so intense it was hard to stand straight, deafening thunder and blinding lightning.

"The power to destroy. To conquer. To make the worlds bow."

"I can't let that happen," I said. "You know I can't."

He laughed in that kind of villainous cartoony way, and I cocked my head, startled by the absurdity of it all. "You're so pathetic," I said. "I thought you were so cool, so edgy and different. But you're just a geeky kid who's lashing out because things haven't gone your way. It's sad. Truly. You feel so entitled so power that you don't even realize how absurd you are." With each word I took a step closer until I knew if I reached my hand out I would touch him... and his staff.

I had no idea what I was doing. I just knew, no matter the cost, he had to be stopped.

And I was pretty sure what that cost would be.

I closed my eyes and silently apologized to Callie for being the world's biggest dick. I apologized to Uncle Sly for disobeying his rules and going where I wasn't allowed.

And then, I lunged.

My plan was simple.

Grab the staff and slam the crystal glowy bit against the wall, thus crushing it.

Easy peasy.

But Devon didn't want to let go.

He roared with fury and yanked back, pulling me off my feet.

But I anticipated that, and didn't resist the pull. Instead, I used it to give me momentum in lunging forward. I swiped my leg under his, causing him to crash down with me on top of him, while simultaneously pushing the staff to the side and using my own head to slam the crystal into the ground.

My vision went white.

An explosion that seemed at once soundless and encompassing all the noise in the world burst forth around us.

Devon screamed, but I couldn't hear his voice, only saw his mouth open in agony as the power that had been pulsing in him burst free of the confines of his body. Bits of my boyfriend sprayed all over me, but it didn't matter, because my end was coming.

I thought I'd broken the crystal ball against my head and the ground. But I'd only cracked it.

That had caused the explosion.

Now, the cracks continued.

Leaking more unstable magic into the environment around me.

Crashing into the walls and ceilings.

Boulders fell.

Dirt smothered me.

I considered running, but my body wouldn't follow my commands.

So I closed my eyes.

Breathing in dirt.

Breathing until I couldn't breathe anymore.

Feeling the weight of the earth drive out the air in my body. Crushing my internal organs. Crushing bones.

I could hear them snap.

Feel them break.

But I could not scream.

Could not cry out.

Could only endure the pain.

And the end came.

I had a fraction of a moment when I felt my heart burst inside my chest, and then there was nothing.

* * *

THE NOTHING GAVE way to a heaviness that was almost unbearable. I had been floating, it seemed, into the ethers of eternity. Now, I was corporeal once again, and standing in the dungeons, or what was left of the dungeons.

I looked down at my body, shocked, confused. I had died. I was sure of it.

Devon was dead.

84

The staff destroyed.

The caverns and older parts of the dungeons appeared to be gone as well, now just a crater of electric fire.

The newer parts of the dungeon still stood, and I had to assume the rest of the Black Lotus was intact.

I waited, knowing my uncle would be here in 3, 2, 1...

"What in tarnations is going on down here?" he asked, standing beside me as if appearing from smoke, his long purple robes pristine.

"I... " I looked at him, and then threw myself into his arms and cried. I didn't stop crying for some time, and it took a lot of deciphering for him to get the story out of me.

When I was done confessing, I looked up at him with swollen eyes. "How am I alive?" I asked.

He brushed my hair out of my face and smiled kindly, gently, with some sadness I didn't understand. "You were blessed by the Mother Dryad as an infant. You can Renew, but only once a day."

"So...I can't die?" There was so much to unpack in this new information I didn't even know where to begin.

"Well, you can, if you're not careful. If you're killed twice before your Renewal regenerates. And there are some forces that can kill you the first time, even with Renewal, but those are very rare indeed."

"Why have you never told me?" I asked.

"I wanted you to take care of this life you have. It's not to be trifled with. Youth these days already think they're immortal, I didn't want to feed that."

I sniffled and wiped at a stray tear. "I'm sorry. I didn't know what he was going to do. I thought he loved me."

Uncle Sly hugged me again. "Oh my child, there is nothing to forgive. This is the age of heartbreak and self-discovery, though... " he looked at the wreckage and frowned. "That doesn't usually involve powerful ancient magics and the destruction of my dungeons."

I chuckled at that, then remembered what I'd done and frowned again. "What do we do now?"

He led me through the dungeons and back into the Black Lotus to his private office. On the way, he called for tea and food and we found it waiting for us by the time we arrived. He tucked me into a blanket made of the softest material in all the worlds—though he would never tell me what it was— and gave me tea and cookies. "Rest. I will handle the rest. The delegates from Nirandel have some explaining to do. In the meantime, I think there's someone who misses you and would like to keep you company."

Callie walked in sheepishly, her head down, her hair curling around her perfect face.

I started crying again, and she rushed to me, holding me as we both apologized and hugged and cried together.

I told her everything.

She told me her stories.

And Uncle Sly filled a new cell in the dungeon with a Nirandel traitor who brought Devon over to fulfill this nefarious quest.

Uncle Sly told me the crystal came from Avakiri. That it was an ancient power that needed protection.

That it was too unstable to ever be channeled by anyone, regardless of their intentions.

That I was lucky to be alive.

IRIS

*S*trong hands pull me out of rubble. His hands.

"You still alive?" he asks, with a small bit of irony.

I choke out dirt and dig out of the mound that buried me, standing beside him. Most of the cavern has collapsed and water is now rushing in from the ocean, but Arias has that under control. It stops before it gets to us, as if an invisible wall holds it there.

I can hear the storm continue to tear through the world outside, and in here it isn't much better. The memories from my past push into the present, shaping what I see. What I understand. What I know.

"I've seen this before," I scream as we look for a way back to the surface. But our path has been blocked by falling stone, trapping us and forcing us to go deeper in.

Totally not the direction I want to be heading, FYI.

"That's impossible," the Rider says, swerving as a rock nearly knocks him in the head.

"When I was sixteen. This kind of power was trapped in a

crystal. Nearly killed me." I consider. "Actually, it did kill me. It was my first death."

My first death. Huh. Not a lot of people get to say that.

Let's just take a moment to marvel at what I can do.

Okay, back to the present catastrophic event.

Because this is truly catastrophic.

If this is the same power, and I can feel in bones it is, then this village is in danger. And I can only die once and come back. This thing could kill me more than that, I fear.

And I have way too much shit on my to-do list for that to happen.

Another boulder nearly crushes Arias and I push him out of the way with my body, saving his ass.

Then he pulls me aside as a lightning bolt strikes the area I was just standing, saving my ass. Okay fine. We're even. Sort of.

And then we step into a cavern that is the size of a base-ball field. In the center is a metal orb made of what looks like trimantium. And it's pulsing with electricity and sending bolts of lightning everywhere. My hair stands on end and my skin glows white from the proximity.

What I felt before, in the Black Lotus dungeons…. That was nothing. That was a raindrop compared to a tsunami.

This is the tsunami.

"We're screwed," I say. "I faced this power once. But only a sliver of it, I realize now. Uncle Sly said it came from Avakiri."

"This is the fifth Spirit. The Storm that could tear apart the worlds. This island has deposits of trimantium through-out, and this cavern is lined with it. It helps stabilize the power. And that center sphere traps the magick here. It was created by the Ancient Ones back when the Storm first ravaged Avakiri, nearly destroying it. It should be stable. I don't know why it's responding like this right now. It never has before."

He covers his face with a pale hand, then looks back at the ball of raging storm ready to destroy us. "Something triggered it. My guess is the Tempest."

I look back, and the path we came down has completely collapsed into itself. Cracks in the stone above us begin to leak as the ocean pushes in to the cavern. We don't have much time.

As if we don't have big enough problems, an explosion shakes the cavern, freeing more stone and dirt and creating cracks in the foundation of the ocean. "What was that?" I ask as I brace myself against a wall while dodging another lightning bolt.

Arias closes his eyes, frowning, and the water pooling at our feet swirls and shifts. Outside, the sounds of explosion escalate. The Rider flinches in his trance, then his eyes pop open. "We're under attack!"

"What? Now? Again?"

"Yes. We need to get out of here."

"The village can't withstand another attack on top of a storm. It must be the Tempest. He's come back for the Spirit."

"Kill me," I say.

"What?"

"Kill me. I will Renew on land and will run to the village to warn everyone. You deal with the Tempest or whatever until I get back. You have your Druid powers, so you should be fine."

He smirks. "Yes, I'll be fine, thanks for worrying."

He holds his sword up. "Are you sure about this?"

"Yes, do it fast, before I get blasted by lightning again."

I close my eyes and wait for the blow. The Rider is fast and precise, and as the metal pierces my heart, killing me, I Renew on the shore, overlooking the ocean.

The protrusion of rocks that form the underground cave are crumbling, and Arias's turquoise sea creature slithers through the debris, filling the water and growing in size. Lightning is escaping the cavern, adding to the storm in the sky, complete with graying clouds and thunder. In the distance, a ship is poised and ready, and as I squint to get a better look, a cannon comes hurling at the shore, landing in the sand with an explosion.

Is this the Tempest? I can't tell.

I sprint towards the shoreline as the water breaks and the head of the sea creature surfaces with the Rider on its back. He uses his magic to shape the water around him into a bridge that he walks across to join me on land. "Those ships are from Inferna. They are Princess Aya's." He looks crossly at me, as if I caused this.

"Then let's just talk to them," I say, my heart skipping a beat at the thought of Elias being here. Of seeing him again. Holding him. "If they see I'm okay, and that the queen is here, they'll have no reason to fight. Your people will be safe. At least from them. The storm is another matter."

Another cannon ball flies overhead, landing behind us in fire and destruction, shattering several trees that lined the shore.

"They don't look like they're here to talk," he says.

I can't completely argue with him, but… "There's got to be a way. If they're here to save me?"

"What makes you so sure they're here for you?" he asks.

I pause at that. I just assumed. "Why else would they be here?"

At that, the wind around us increases, ripping into foliage and riling up the water into a frenzy of unsteady waves. Thunder drowns out our voices for a moment as lightning cuts through the sky. The dark clouds hovering above continue the deluge of rain pouring over us, obscuring our vision.

Even the Rider, in all his meticulously chosen armor, looks like nothing more than a drowned rat in this weather.

"There is great power on this island. We've kept it hidden for centuries. Until today," he says.

"This is the first time anyone's been here?" I ask, incredulous.

"Yes. And now we have been attacked twice in as many nights." Again, he glares at me like it's my fault. "You must have pulled Elias here with your power."

"Well, buddy, you're the one who dragged me here in the first place, so check yourself before casting blame." I stick a finger in his chest for good measure, and he looks annoyed and bemused simultaneously.

"It is true. I have wrought havoc on my people. I must protect the Storm Spirit. You have to go to the village and warn my parents. Tell them to get the people to safety. All are in danger, both from the attack and the storm. They will already be preparing for the storm, but won't know about the attack."

That's fabulous. "So, no to the diplomatic resolution? They are the good guys, remember."

He frowns as another bolt of lightning splits a tree near us. "You overestimate my brother. He is a villain who has committed heinous acts. He has no code. He is not like you."

"And you haven't?" I say.

"Much of my misdeeds are rumors, lies and speculation. I am not as evil as you would like to imagine me, nor am I good. I am necessary. That is all I can claim. I have done what needs doing for the greater good."

"Funny, he would say the same about himself. You two are more alike than you give yourself credit for."

He pauses, as if he's going to say more but changes his mind. "Go, warn the others. I will handle my siblings."

I'm torn. On the one hand, I totes have to save the innocent. That's like my whole job description basically. On the other hands, I don't want Arias hurting Elias or Aya. They don't know what's going on here. Someone needs to talk them down, and it sure as hell isn't going to be the Rider.

But…

Shit.

Innocent people verses my boyfriend and his sister.

Damnit. Of course I have to save the innocent.

Arias could have killed his brother, but didn't. And I've seen there's some good in him.

I grab the Rider's arm and squeeze. "Don't kill them. Fight if you must. But try to talk. Try to explain. I will warn Kayla and Tavian and then I'll be back. Do. Not. Kill."

"It is not my intention to kill," he says, which does not reassure me in the least.

"Make it your intention *not* to kill anyone, mmkay?"

I accept his half-assed nod as the best I am going to get, and then I run inland, hoping I remember my way in the rain and darkness.

I need to find the Rider's parents. And I needed a way to communicate with Elias so that he will not do the thing he's about to do. I know him. I know he won't forgive himself if he hurts the people of this village.

Whether it's to save me or for some other reason.

There has to be a better way.

And I am going to find it.

As I slip and slide through a tropical forest searching for the most direct path to the village, I don't hear the enemy chasing me until it's too late.

The storm covers his tracks too well.

When he approaches, it is with doom and malice.

And I fear the worst.

A demon.

A blood sucker.

Then *he* shows up.

The destroyer of worlds.

The butcher of armies.

The —

Oh, it's only Imenath. Sorry, I thought it was actually someone dangerous.

"We meet again," screams Imenath, stepping forward from behind a tree, his entire body covered in silver armor resembling a skeleton. His face masked behind a helmet sprouting horns. He carries his giant spiked mace on his hip and grips it with his hand.

"Imenath?"

"Imenath the Great has returned for you, Watcher!"

Lightning blazes in the sky, striking at the tree next to me, which groans as it prepares itself to collapse.

I'm about to hop out of the way when Imenath plows into me, knocking the air out of my lungs and landing on top of me in all his—very heavy—armor.

"Get. Off. Of. Me." I push and strain until he rolls over, then sit up, panting, wet, covered in mud now, thanks a lot for that. "What are you doing here, buddy? How… " I'm perplexed. How did he hop worlds and find me on a secret island? This dude might be more useful than I gave him credit for. "I can't fight you right now. I'm on a pretty important mission and a lot of people's lives are at stake."

"I came here not to fight the great Watcher, but to save her. I am your hero! Your knight in shining armor!" He puffs out his chest to show how shiny his armor indeed is. "Fear not, Watcher, Imenath the Great is here! See? I have already saved you from this ferocious and terrifying tree! Now I shall save you from your kidnappers."

I try not to laugh. I swear I do. And I think I cover it well, what with the thunder and storm raging and all. He doesn't notice. Instead, he sees me smile. "You're amazing, dude. Truly." I groan as I stand and brush off what I can of the gunk. This white outfit isn't going to survive. "But right now, I don't need saving, I need to do the saving. We have to warn the village. We're being attacked and there's an unstable power on the loose here."

Imenath roars into the storm. "I am greater than any powers. And that ship is here to help. I snuck on to it and came here, secret like. Imenath is truly a master of stealth."

"I'm genuinely impressed. But can we walk and talk? I gotta get to the village stat, dude. And this storm is making my progress slow."

Imenath reaches into the bag tied around his waist and pulls out something small and fluffy. "Imenath also brought Watcher's trusty companion."

"Theo!" My eyes fill with tears as the little ball of wet fur meows at me plaintively, clearly unhappy with his current circumstances. I grab him and hug him close to me.

"You did good, Imenath. Great, even! When this is all said and done, there might be a place for you with the Hunters. What do you think of that?"

His eyes widen and joy fills his face. "Truly?"

"Truly!" I set Theo down and give him a look he knows well. The tiny meow turns to a mighty growl as Theo shifts from pint-sized to Manticore, gray and white fur turning gold, wings growing from his back. "Now, let's get to the village and save the innocent!"

I hop onto my baby, so happy to see him and have him here finally, and Imenath joins me as we take to the sky.

ELIAS

The sun has set when we are close enough to see the shores of the island that match the coordinates Callie gave me.

Aya has been preoccupied with her crew, so we haven't discussed our strategy for approaching shore.

When a cannon launches from our ship and explodes on the sand a distance from us, I realize she decided the strategy without me.

I can see someone at the edge of the ocean. A woman in white. But then my focus is pulled towards an outcropping of rocks, where a giant sea creature is emerging.

Can it be? Does the Water Druid live here?

I holler for Aya's men to cease fire as I seek her out, but she is nowhere to be found. Smaller boats have already left the ship with members of the crew on them. "Where's my sister?" I ask one of the men. He shrugs. "Dunno. She be telling us to bomb the place, then loot and riot. My boys be more than happy to oblige," he says, grinning with a mostly toothless smile.

This makes no sense. If Iris is on the island, we can't just blow it up. We might kill her. Plus, there are likely innocent people living here. Why didn't she consult me? Why are we going to war without knowing the facts first? Facts such as whether or not she's actually here, or are we just bombing an innocent village, or both?

There are too many missing pieces, and I can't wrap my head around it all. Her approach makes no sense, which is probably why she didn't tell me about it. I shout at the crew once again to cease fire, but they ignore me, too caught up in their blood lust.

I search the ship—and her private quarters—seeking my sister, but do not find her. So Duke and I slip away from the men and take a small boat, making our way to shore as far away from their war party as we can. I don't want to be seen with them. I want to find out what's going on first.

The water is brackish and the storm makes paddling difficult. Taking a roundabout way also adds time and tedium to the journey, and we are both soaked to the bone when we dock on the white sand.

At first glance, it's a beautiful place, especially so if the weather wasn't destroying it.

At sea, the Water Spirit coils around the rocks it first appeared near, pulling someone out of the water. The warrior raises his hands and rides the water, maneuvering it to his will.

That must be the Water Druid. But on closer inspection, it looks like...

No. It can't be.

Arias, the White Rider, is also the Water Druid?

I'm stunned. Frozen in place. If Arias is here, then Iris must be as well.

At the far end of the shore, some men have made it to the beach and will begin their raiding.

There are likely people here who must be warned.

But I have to capture Arias and find out what happened to Iris.

I look to him, and then inland to where I assume a village would dwell.

I see smoke rising from fires, so I know my assumptions are right.

I must choose which path to take.

Callie told me to seek the truth and not the easy lie. Could my brother be the easy lie right now? What is the truth?

Iris would protect the people.

The hardened part of me would go after my brother and make him pay for nearly killing me twice and kidnapping Iris.

I turn inland and begin to run.

* * *

DUKE IS MORE surefooted than myself as we traverse the tropical forest that separates the village from the ocean. But I hold my own, as my sword slaps against my hip, ready for battle and blood.

I hope it doesn't come to that.

I'm here to fight the Rider, not my sister's men, and not innocent villagers.

As I make my way inland I hear the sounds of life, of people, of children.

Just as I feared.

How did my sister know there would be people to attack? Why would she do this without talking with me first?

I make fast time and arrive at the village before Aya's men.

The village already looks like it's been attacked. Which

makes no sense. But huts have been destroyed, people are injured. What's going on here?

A child cries out and points to the sky and I look up just in time to see a giant Manticore landing in the middle of the village, with Iris on his back.

"Iris!" My voice carries over the voices and Iris looks my way, her face beatific as it breaks out in smile.

"Elias!" She slides off Theo and comes running. Some kind of demon dude awkwardly falls off behind her and raises his sword by way of greeting the villagers.

Duke, for his part, gives a happy wag at Iris, but heads straight for Theo, as they play and greet each other.

But my thoughts are completely consumed by only one person as Iris throws herself into my arms and I catch her and hold her tightly. I never want to let go of this woman. Being without her, not knowing how she fared, it nearly broke me.

I bury my face in her shoulder, her hair tickling my nose. She's covered in mud and as wet as everyone else in this storm, and as the rain pelts us I kiss her deeply.

When we part, she cups my face. "I've missed you. I thought you were dead." Her voice breaks at that.

"I'm a hard man to kill. You of all people should know that," I say with a grin.

She sighs in exaggerated exacerbation. "Seriously. How did I get this blood thirsty reputation? I. Don't. Kill. Trust me, Prince, if I'd wanted you dead, you'd be dead."

I chuckle at that. I've missed our banter. "Oh really?"

She winks. "Really. You're just lucky that goes against my code."

"I love you for your code," I say, the words coming out more serious and emotion-laden than I intended.

Her eyes widen and she kisses me again, a quick kiss that sends a jolt of desire through me. But there's no time for that now. "My sister is attacking this village. I thought to save you, but now I don't know. She's disappeared and her men won't listen to me. We have to protect the people."

Iris nods and pulls away from my arms. "I'm glad you're here to help."

She turns as two familiar people walk up. I raise an eyebrow. "Kayla? Tavian? What are you doing here?"

They look at each other and shrug. "It's a long story, one that will have to wait until after this is dealt with."

The sky rumbles with thunder and a great lightning bolt too big to be natural strikes at the center of the village, setting huts afire even in the rain, and cracking open the earth. "What kind of storm is this?" I ask, having to shout to be heard.

Iris grabs my hand. "I'll explain on the way. Kayla, you and Tavian help the people and get them to safety, if there is such a thing right now. Use Imenath, he can help. Elias and I will go assist Arias."

Everyone seems comfortable following Iris's command, which doesn't surprise me at all. This woman has a way of leading that would make a king envious. We jog over to Theo and Duke who are playing in the mud together.

Iris laughs and gives a hug to the great wolf. "Good to see you too, buddy. But we've got to get out of here." She climbs onto Theo's back and I join behind her, wrapping my arms around her waist.

I'm just about to ask what we should do about Duke, when he hops up behind me and takes a position on Theo's neck, in front of Iris. She wraps an arm around him and we take to the sky.

I have to scream in her ear to be heard, but this is too important to wait. "Why are we helping the White Rider? Isn't he the enemy?"

"It's complicated," she says. "You'll see."

We fly back to the ocean as Aya's men are clamoring up the shoreline to pillage the town and wreak havoc on the people there. By the rocks that jut out past the surf, a figure dressed in black armor with a gold helmet faces off against the White Rider, his serpent spiraling around them.

Theo hovers over the crew and begins picking them off four at a time, one for each giant claw, disemboweling them and tossing them into the water. It doesn't take him long to eviscerate the entire crew, save the ones left on the ship who are not shy about loosing their cannons on us.

"Bloody hell, good work, Theo!" I scream over the howling winds.

Duke jumps off his friend and picks off any of Theo's victims still left, then howls into the night as Theo carries Iris and I across the waters to the rocks where the worst of the storm seems to be centered.

"There's a fifth Spirit," Iris screams. "The Storm Spirit. That's the Tempest, the one you've been seeking, and he's trying to claim the Storm Spirit for himself, but it's unstable. It will destroy the worlds. We have to stop him. That's what Arias has been trying to do all along. Stop the Tempest and protect the Spirit."

Her explanation, choppy as it is over wind and storm and thunder, slides some pieces together I didn't know I was missing.

It's still hard for me to accept that the White Rider is on our side. But right now, I have to trust her.

And I do. We hop off of Theo and run to join Arias who is locked in battle with the Tempest.

Iris dives into the fight full force and knocks the Tempest off a jutting edge, but the Tempest rises from the sea foam, a cloak of shadow draped around him, defying gravity. He cackles, his voice low and ominous. "You cannot stop me. I will have what I seek. I can feel the power seeking me out even as we speak."

With a thunderous jolt, the rock below us cracks open as lightning tears it apart.

Iris falls from the rocks into the water, and the sea serpent lifts her out as Theo plucks her up and carries her into the sky.

Arias lunges for the Tempest but strikes nothing but shadow as he disappears into nothing, reappearing behind me with a sword to my neck.

"Surrender or he dies."

The White Rider laughs, the shredded white cloth over-laying his white armor dancing behind him in the wind. "You think I care about him. I already slit his throat once. Do it again and see if that matters to me."

"Hey now, let's all talk this through a minute. I quite like my throat where it is, thank you very much," I say as I fall back into the Tempest and use the momentum to pull him over me and slam him into the rocks. At the same time, Iris drops down with Theo, who picks the Tempest up with his claws, but the Tempest once again uses whatever shadow magic he has to vanish, reappearing at the far edge of the rocky cliff. As he does, the lightning from under the ocean rises up and focuses its aim, driving itself into the Tempest's chest.

The Tempest screams, and it is a sound to topple mountains. His body shakes, spasms, and lights up with the glow of a sun exploding in space.

Theo lands next to me and Iris slides off, her sword in hand, eyes fixated on the spectacle before us.

The Tempest's mask cracks as the lightning makes its way through him, and when the light dims and the man falls to the ground, the power of the Storm coursing through his blood, I see through the convenient lie into the truth.

The Tempest was no man at all.
For I stand staring at the face of my sister, Aya.

IRIS

"*A*ya?" Elias stands, his dark hair whipping in the wind, as he faces his sister.

I'm personally too shell-shocked to have a witty comeback to this. I mean, give me a sec and I'll come up with one, but daaaymmmnn what the hell? My girl has been pulling the evil strings all along?

I think of Ari in the cave, her mind a wreck, and I can't even with it all. Aya did that to her own mother? How? Why?

"How? Why?" Elias says, echoing my thoughts.

Aya stands as electricity zaps through her. Her fingertips shoot lightning and her hair stands on end, vibrating with the power she now embodies. She raises her arms and spreads them, letting the wind and storm grow in her as it pulls her from the rocks and she hovers in the air staring down at us.

"Our parents were weak," she says. "They have everything. The Midnight Star. The Earth Spirit. And still they relied on puny words and outdated ideas to create peace. I longed for a Spirit of my own, a way to claim enough power to do what needs to be done to ensure our people enjoy the peace and prosperity they deserve. And now, as queen and as the Storm Spirit, I will ensure it. For us, and for all the worlds."

Arias steps forward, holding his sword out, like that's going to do anything at all. A for effort though, buddy. "You cannot control this Spirit, Aya. It will control you and destroy everyone you love. You must release it. Give it back to be safeguarded."

Aya laughs, and the storm ravaging the island grows as her power does. "Give it back? After all that I've done to acquire it? I spent decades infiltrating Lix Tetrax, learning its ways until I discovered the leader. Then I became his apprentice, learning everything I could from him. He had other plans, plans to bring the Unseen Lord to the worlds and blot out the sun. I used his ambition against him and killed him when I was ready to take control. I had pure ambitions. Noble ones. Unlike him. And so I worked, moving his plots forward but for a very different purpose. To discover the location of the Storm Spirit and embrace it into me until I had the power to rule the way our parents should have."

"You can't do this," I say, raising my sword, because, you know, why not. Everyone else is doing it. "I won't let you."

She laughs, and this time it is filled with wind and thunder and lightning. "And who are you to stop me? A weak Unseen Lord who doesn't know her powers and is too restrained by her pathetic code to do anything about it even if you could."

Well that stings.

Still, this little convo bought us time for Theo to do his thing, which is to whip around behind her and attack while we rush her from the front. It has to work. We are three of the most powerful warriors in all the worlds. Surely she can't be that must stronger.

Spoiler. She is.

She blasts Theo out of the sky with lightning and as he

falls into the water I scream and dash at her with my sword. Arias uses his powers to push Theo to shore, saving him from drowning, but my buddy isn't moving. Duke runs to him, licking him, as I fight the Tempest/Aya/wtf?

She blinks into shadow and appears behind Arias, thrusting a sword into his side before blinking away again. His sea creature lets out an anguished sound and slams the ocean water, making waves that come for the Tempest, but again, she disappears into shadow, appearing by Elias. Their swords clash and I run over to back him up, pushing worry over Theo aside. He's okay. He has to be. Right? Just tell me yes, okay. I can't fight if I'm worried about him.

She easily bests Elias, her sword now shooting lightning and electrifying him when they clash. He falls back spasming from the shock.

Well, shit. This isn't looking good for any of us. I make a run for her, using all my best moves. I'd give a lot for my daggers right now. Swords are so clunky and limiting.

But I make do, and we come face to face. It's a well-matched battle. I'm pissed. As pissed as I've ever been. And as I rage, I feel power build in me. Consuming me. We clash, the lightning zapping me, and finding something familiar in me. Like an old friend.

Aya raises a perfectly plucked eyebrow, and again I am mesmerized by her beauty even as she tries to kill me. "My Spirit knows you. You've met before."

"Yeah, it was a hoot. Good times." I knock her sword aside and dodge to the left, leading her to the edge of the cliff. She uses her super-duper annoying shadow trick to disappear and reappear behind me, sinking her blade into my shoulder as she does.

I bite down on the scream and push in instead of away as she's expecting. The move surprises her, since, you know, it's actually embedding her sword deeper into my body and it hurts like a mother effing bitch. But it disorients her enough that I can shove my sword between my rib and arm, into her. I don't hit critical organs, but I do give her a nice hole in her side.

Lightning sizzles around her and her scream turns to a laugh as she looks past me, towards Arias and Elias.

She raises her arms and pulls all the lightning into her, then directs that power against the rocks that we are on, tearing them apart.

Arias and Elias slip into the water, rocks and debris pulling them into the chaotic waves. Theo is still unconscious on shore and Duke can't do much from where he is.

"Choose, Watcher. Me or them." She pulls her sword out of me and absorbs her power into her once again, allowing it to electrify her.

"I can see the weave of the worlds now," she says, apropos of nothing. Her eyes are unfocused and her voice distant. "I can do things I never imagined. Everything will be different now." With a wave of her hand, lightning burns out of her and tears a hole into the night sky, revealing a portal to another world. She looks at me again, her eyes refocusing. "They're dying. Better save them, little Watcher." Then she jumps into the portal and disappears into another world.

I have a split second to make a decision. To try to follow her or save Arias and Elias.

I turn towards shore and dive into the water, avoiding getting knocked out by a rock as best I can. My shoulder throbs and leaks blood into the ocean, and I say a quick prayer that there are no sharks or people eating critters around here. Then I dive again, searching for the Vane Spero brothers.

It's dark. The storm has gotten worse, if you can imagine, which I'm pretty sure you can't, since I couldn't have before this mess. And I cannot see for shit.

But they are dying. I have to find them.

"Elias! Arias!" I scream with a hoarse voice over the tempest. With all the strength I can, I swim, dive, search, and swim some more. I won't give up. I can't. But my strength is fading. My eyes burn with tears of fear and rage. I don't know how to keep going.

And then, out of the corner of my eye, I see something in the water. A shimmering gold tail. A mermaid. The one we saw sunbathing the other day.

She dives deep and pulls someone out of the water. Arias it looks like. It's his armor. Leaving him ashore, she dives again, and I dive with her. I see Elias before she does and grab his arm, pulling against armor and pain and the currents of the water. She joins me, reaching for both of us, and helping us gain traction against the waves. When we reach shore, she hovers in the water, her golden eyes bright, and falling on Arias. "I cannot help more," she says.

"You've helped so much," I say, overcome with emotion. "Thank you. You've saved us all."

She nods, casts one more glance at Arias, and then disappears into the water.

I crawl over to Elias and tip him to the side, using mouth to mouth to clear his lungs. Then I start CPR, as I beg and pray for him to be okay. "Wake up, damnit. I'm not done with you yet."

After a few minutes, he sputters and coughs out a sea of ocean water and I cry hug him. "I thought I'd lost you. Again!"

"Like I said, I'm hard to kill," he chokes, his voice raw.

"Check on your brother, I have to see about Theo."

Elias doesn't look super excited to do mouth to mouth with his twin, but I don't give a shit. We don't have time to be picky here. I stand on wobbly feet and get to my best fur buddy as fast as I can. Duke has been tending to him, but he looks so lifeless, it crushes me.

"Hey Theo. Hey buddy. Wake up. I need you." I pet his head and hug him, rubbing his fur to warm him up. He rumbles, low at first, then louder, and his form shifts into his smaller kitten version. But he opens his eyes, curling into my hands and meows.

My heart nearly bursts with relief. "You okay, little dude?"

He meows again, and I create a makeshift wrap for him to keep him close to my skin, though keeping him dry right now is impossible. We're all so wet I don't even remember what it feels like to be dry.

Elias and Arias walk up, both looking worse for wear. Duke whines and shoves his big head into Elias's hand. He's rewarded with a scratch behind the ears. The giant wolf regards Arias with intrigue and suspicion, sniffing him cautiously.

"We need to get under cover," Arias says. "This storm will only worsen."

He begins to hike inland, and we follow, because where else are we going to go, right?

"I know where Kayla and Tavian would have taken the people. We had a back up plan in place in case the Spirit ever became unstable." He drops his head, rain pouring over it. "I never thought we'd have to use it."

Elias reaches for my hand and I squeeze his. There's so much to talk about. So much to figure out. But 1: it's way too hard to communicate out here and 2: it's not really the time.

So we share a look and keep moving, as Arias leads us to a section of the island I haven't been yet. It's deeper into the jungle, away from the shore and the village. I frown and tug on his sleeve. "What about Ari?"

Elias jerks his head at that. "My mother's here?"

Oops. "Yeah, sorry, I was going to tell you, but... well... " I shrug as if to say, when? When could we have had this conversation?

"Kayla and Tavian would have moved her. She's safe, I assure you. Let's go. We're almost there." Arias is no-nonsense as we move deeper into the jungle. Theo rests against my chest, sleeping and shivering. Duke scouts ahead, sniffing at everything.

It's slow going, slogging through the thick undergrowth of forest that's now heavy with moisture. My feet keep getting stuck in slime so gross I feel like it's crawling up my legs. But eventually we arrive at the mouth of a cave covered by hanging moss that blocks visibility of the entrance. Arias pushes the moss away and invites us in.

For the first time in hours, the rain can't reach us. The inside of the cave is drier the further in we travel. I shiver at the memory of recently being buried alive, and Elias wraps an arm around me. "Cold?"

"Traumatized," I say, and recount the story.

He raises an eyebrow. "So now I know two of your greatest fears. What's the third?"

I snort. "Nice try. You'll have to wait on that one."

Let's just hope I'm never in a position to tell him.

It's the worst one.

The cave is spacious, the stalactites so high above us I'd have to ride Theo to reach them.

As we walk further, I hear the echoes of others at a distance. Then closer, until we reach a cavern filled with those who made it from the village.

There's a huge fire built in the center, where people are warming themselves, and smaller fires scattered throughout for families to converge around.

I scan the crowd and see Kayla administering healing to those who need her. When she sees us, she heads towards us, her face constricted in worry. "What happened?"

Arias frowns. "Nothing good. Where's Tavian?"

As if summoned, he joins us from the shadows, nodding a greeting at Elias.

"Is there somewhere more private we can talk?" Arias asks.

Kayla leads us through the cavern, whereupon I see that accommodations have been made for a longer term stay. Beds are laid, small fires already have pots hanging over them for food, and children are distracted by dolls and games.

I look for Lala and her family, but don't see them immediately, and we turn a corner into a more private section of the cave, one where it seems Kayla and Tavian have set up their quarters. We sit on furs around a fire as Tavian passes out blankets for us to dry ourselves with while we explain what happened.

At the end, no one looks thrilled. Dejected is a more apt description.

"There's something we need to tell you," Kayla says softly. She's speaking to all of us, but looking straight at Arias.

Oh shit. Whatever it is, it's heavy.

"What?" Arias asks, his jaw hardening.

"When you died," Kayla beings, "it was… it devastated all of us. Especially your parents."

Arias makes a move to interrupt and Kayla holds up her hand. "Your birth parents. They were heartbroken. We all were. When you rose from the dead with your powers, we discovered you because even as an infant you were strong. You inadvertently devastated a village, trying to find home."

Arias sucks in a breath, and Elias and I stay silent.

"We realized then that you had the Water Spirit, and we feared a prophesy had come to pass."

"What prophesy," he asks through gritted teeth.

"That a High Fae born of the Druid Spirit would destroy the world. It was a prophesy told to Arianna on her wedding night. If anyone had found out you lived, and carried the Water Spirit, they would have killed you out of fear. That is why Tavian and I raised you in secret. We thought it would be the safest for you, and that we could help you learn to control your powers."

Double shit. Because you see where this is going, right?

"But I'm not the one spoken of in the prophesy, am I?" he asks, pain in his voice.

Kayla's head drops, and Tavian places a hand on hers and speaks. "No. It would appear you're not. Aya is."

"So my whole life was a lie for nothing."

"You still would have been in danger. Constantly. I don't know that we could have kept you alive until adulthood," Kayla says. "So it wasn't for nothing. It was because we all loved you so much that we were willing to do anything to protect you. Don't you see that? Your mother and father were willing to lose you... again. That tore out their heart. We were willing to leave our lives and family to live in isolation, because we loved you so much. That is how much you were always loved, Arias. All of us gave up everything out of love for you."

Arias looks away, squeezing his eyes shut, and I reach out a hand and place it on his shoulder. I don't have words to offer, but I can at least offer this kindness.

After a long, silent moment, Arias clears his throat. "We can't defeat her, not without the Shadow's Bane," Arias says. "She's too strong now."

All right then, back to business. He definitely needs time to process this.

"You have the Twilight Bow, after you stole it from us," Elias accuses.

He nods. "And I still have it. Good thing I took it, or it would likely have ended up with the Moonlight Sword. Locked up by the Council. Out of reach."

"Whatever," I say, channeling my inner mopey teen. "So we need the Shadow Mantle and the Moonlight Sword. But we aren't going to get the sword this time. They learned from their mistakes. And we have no idea where the mantle is."

"I know where you can get a Moonlight Sword," Kayla says. "It's not the same one. But they are the same."

My eyes widen. "There are *two?*"

Kayla nods. "I forged the second one myself. For Ari."

Well, shit. "Guess it's time to talk to your mother," I tell Elias.

We leave Duke and Theo by the fire to rest and warm. Kayla excuses herself to continue tending to the wounded. "There are many," she says. "The storm ravaged the village and killed some, wounded more. Even if we are to stop this, the people here won't quickly recover from the devastation wrought."

"And the storm, it's just going to keep at it?" I ask.

Arias shakes his head. "Worse. It's going to escalate until it destroys everything in its path, and then it will move on to another world."

"Lovely."

We follow Tavian through the tunnels to where Ari is being kept. "What happened to her? Why are you imprisoning her?" Elias asks with a hard edge to his voice.

"She's cursed," Arias says. "By the Tempest."

"Likely excuse. You've been wanting to punish her for abandoning you your whole life. I'm supposed to believe this bullshit story?"

I lay a hand on his arm. "She tried to kill me, Elias. It's true. The Tempest is affecting her mind."

That quiets him, and I worry at his reaction when he sees the state she's in.

I wasn't wrong to worry either.

He's furious.

"You have her shackled? Chained up like a monster?" He rushes to her side. "Mother. What have they done?"

But all the great queen can do is rock back and forth, mumbling. Her eyes are sunken and dark, her skin sallow. She hasn't eaten the food laid out for her. I'm glad I at least was able to bathe and dress her, and I see they brought her bedding, but it still must be a shocking sight for Elias.

There's pain in his voice when he speaks again. "How do we free her from this?" he asks, heartbroken.

"We must kill the Tempest," Arias says.

"You mean my sister," Elias says. "To save my mother I must kill my sister."

Arias crosses his arms over his chest. "You must kill your sister to save all the Nine Worlds, and yes, your mother will be saved as well."

Ari's moaning grows louder and her back and forth rocking increases in speed and urgency. All eyes return to her as we look on helplessly, not sure what to do.

I reach out and take her hand. "Arianna. I think you can still hear me. We need your sword so we can save you and your people from a great destruction. Can you tell us where it is?"

She squeezes my hand so tightly my bones grind together, but says nothing.

I'm about to leave her when a voice crashes into my mind. "Ask the mermaids!"

Arianna is speaking to me again, mentally.

"What?" I ask. "What does that mean?"

"Ask the mermaids!" she says again, then she slumps over and whimpers into her fur bed. Her voice in my head is silenced.

I look at Elias and Arias with a small bit of hope. "She spoke to me," I say. "Like she did before."

Arias looks confused, and I realize he doesn't know about

the communication. Ah well. He doesn't need all our secrets explained.

"What did she say?" asks Elias.

"She said, 'ask the mermaids.' Do either of you know what that means?"

Arias frowns. "Yes, I'm afraid I do."

IRIS

*A*rias confers briefly with Kayla and Tavian, then gestures for us to follow. Theo and Duke try to join, but Arias shakes his head. "They can't come where we're going."

I give Theo some love. "Sorry buddy, not this time."

Elias pats Duke's head and asks, "Where *are* we going?"

It's clear from his tone he hasn't moved into the #Team-Arias camp, and I don't totally blame him. I mean, it wasn't that long ago that dude slit his throat and left him for dead. I'd be bitter too. And he hasn't seen his brother in the same light I have.

As we head to the entrance of the cave, where the sound of the storm is frightful, I moan. "Do we *have* to go out there again? I was just stating to feel my toes again."

"Yes, we *have* to go out there again," Arias says with a mocking tone I so do not appreciate. "But we won't be in the storm long."

"That's a relief," I say, cheered by that thought at least.

"We'll be underwater," he says, then steps outside.

"Wait, what now?"

I get a total of zero of my questions answered while we once again hike through sludge and wet puddles. He feigns not being able to hear me, but I think it's really just him blowing me off. Brat.

When we arrive at shore, it's clear the storm is escalating. Chunks of the cliffs overlooking the ocean have collapsed into the water. The waves are growing at alarming rates and the island looks like it's taken a severe beating. I'm not sure how they will restore this place, if we can ever stop the storm.

Arias tells us to stand by the water. "Be ready to jump in when I tell you. You won't be able to breathe out of water."

"Hold up now," Elias says, but it's too late. Arias waves his hands, works some Water Druid voodoo and whoosh! I can no longer breathe good 'ol oxygen. Well, shit.

I jump in, submerging my head, but now what? I still can't breathe. Dude might have given a bit more instruction.

His sea serpent appears and Arias speaks under water, like it's totally normal. "Grab on to him. And breathe, you imbeciles."

A few more minutes and I won't have a choice, so I grab on to some scales and take a tiny tentative breath. I'm totally ready to cough up some serious sea water, but instead, I find I can breathe just fine. "What did you do?" I ask, amazed I can speak underwater.

"I gave you the temporary ability to breathe underwater, obviously. Now let's go. My Water Spirit will take us to the kingdom of the mer-people. Be quiet and let me do all the talking. They don't like strangers and have been known to eat them."

"Ugh. Been there, done that, and I'm not keen to die that way again."

Arias raises an eyebrow. "Mer-People ate you?"

I shake my head. "Witches. Boiled alive for supper. I was quite delicious I'm told."

Elias snorts, making a sound for the first time in this whole convo.

It's a long swim down to the bottom of the ocean, and it gets cold, but at the point where it's almost unbearable, Arias uses his powers to heat us up, and I sigh in relief. "You could have done that in the storm," I accuse. He just shrugs. Cheeky bastard.

We pass sights to behold. I don't know shit about under-water things, so let's just say there are some really cool seafood like creatures of all colors and shapes and levels of spiky scaliness. And some beautiful floaty plant life. Really cool. I'd like to do this again when I'm not mid-apocalypse.

When the Mer-Kingdom comes into view, it takes my breath away. The castle is stunning, made of white and peach marbled shell that glistens in the water, with a beautiful undersea garden surrounding it. It's dazzling.

But not as dazzling as the divine mer-people swimming throughout. Men, women, even children, with fins in a variety of colors that match their hair and eyes. Wow!

As they see us approach, they form a kind of reception line. They ooh and ahh over Arias, but when they start sniffing me and Elias, I lay my palm on my sword. I am not going to be fish food.

"Don't provoke them," Arias says with a stern voice. "You will not win. They can be vicious."

"Why are they nice to you?" I ask, holding tightly to the sea creature's scales.

"Because I'm the Water Druid. That's a tremendous power in their eyes. And I've been the ambassador from the island in the past. You're just interlopers."

"I see."

I finally see a face I recognize, the mermaid from the

rocks who helped save our lives. I smile at her, and she smiles back, her teeth sharp and deadly. She swims over and joins us. "Thank you," I say again.

She nods, then addresses Arias. "Why are you here, Great One?"

"We wish to speak to your queen."

The mermaid frowns. "For you I can do this. But for them… "

"Please. It's vital they are there as well. This is a matter of life and death. For all, not just the earth walkers."

She nods. "Very well, release all weapons and follow me."

Elias and I are super reluctant to give up what little protection we have, but Arias glares at us until we drop everything and follow the mermaid. She seems to command a lot of respect, and I notice atop her head sits a crown made of shells. "Who is she?" I whisper to Arias.

"The daughter of the queen. Princess Lindora."

Oh shit. We were rescued by a mermaid princess? That's a new one for my books.

The sea serpent shrinks as we are ushered into the castle. There are no floors within sight of the queen, who sits in a throne that floats in the water, so Arias uses his powers to create a platform of water for us to stand, though he quickly has us kneel.

"Royal Mother, Queen Korella, may I present the Water Druid and his companions, who seek an audience with you."

Queen Korella is striking, with a crown made of elaborately designed shell. Her hair, fin and eyes are a deep purple with splashes of royal blue and her skin shines turquoise. She looks down on us with a frown. "What have you come here seeking, Druid?"

Arias rises, and Elias and I follow suit. "Great Queen, we come begging your favor, that you would release the Moonlight Sword to us, once left in your care by our own Queen Arianna."

Guards stand around her and several other mer-people swim about, watching in wonder. She flicks her hand. "Clear the room. Guards may stay."

The princess looks up, surprised, but leaves with everyone else, until it's only us and the guards left.

"And why should I do you this favor? When was the last time your people helped us? And now, you have set the Great Storm free, disturbing our kingdom and threatening the oceans we dwell in."

As the queen speaks, I notice an odd flick of light playing on her features. A shift in her eye color or the shape of her nose. I study her more carefully as Arias answers, using my growing abilities to see her more clearly.

"Great One, if I have neglected our allies in the sea, I apologize. You have only to ask and we are at your service. But this threat poses a risk to all kinds, and without this sword, our worlds may both be swallowed up by the storms to come."

By the time Arias is done, I see the truth. I see past the illusion the queen is using.

I summon my power and my supernatural speed and strength, and push off, pulling out my hidden blade as I do. With reflexes that surprise even me, I am at the queen's side with a knife to her throat.

Arias looks ready to throttle me. Elias looks amused.

The guards look nervous.

"Reveal yourself, Marasphyr."

Why Marasphyr, the mermaid who spends considerable time at the Black Lotus, is here posing as queen, I have no clue. But I will find out.

The queen smiles and drops her illusion. Arias gasps. Elias looks smug on my behalf. Proud, even. He's adorable.

"Bravo," she says, clapping. "You are the first to figure it out."

I look at the guards, my blade still at her neck. "What are you waiting for? Arrest her!"

Marasphyr looks sternly at them. "Leave us." They do so without pause.

What the—?.

Then Marasphyr turns into shadow and reappears behind Iris. "The guards know I am filling in as a replacement," she says, her lips close to my ear, my blade now pointed at nothing.

I spin to face her. "Why? What happened to the real queen?"

Marasphyr shrugs. "She died. I am filling in until her heir comes of age."

"Princess Lindora?" I ask.

"The same."

I frown. "She looks old enough to me."

Marasphyr smiles. "Our people have different rules. One must be very old and wise to sit on the throne. It must be earned with wisdom and maturity. I've never understood humans with their worship of blood above reason. To sit a child on the throne, it's ridiculous. Even vampires rush to it, when they particularly don't need to. The mer-people have the way of it."

Marasphyr swims to the side, bringing the brothers into our discussion. "Now that we are alone and have that business out of the way, we can speak frankly." She moves her hand and the side of the throne room changes. The water beyond the glass becomes clear, revealing the Moonlight Sword hanging in light.

"I will give you the sword, but first, I need something in return."

"Like what?" I ask, knowing there's always a catch with her.

"A promise."

Yeah, it's as bad as I thought. Worse, actually. Nothing spelled out. No details. This never ends well.

"A promise that when I have need of you, you shall come to my aid," she says.

Arias answers without hesitation. "Very well."

"No," says Marasphyr, pointing to me. "I want her and her alone to swear. The promise will be bound to her."

Shit. Double shit. But crap, what choice to I have? The apocalypse has sent a calling card and is on its way. Unless I get this sword, we're screwed. "I promise," I say, reluctantly. And with those fated words I feel the magical tether binding us together as a new mark appears on my hand, creating a fresh line where my old mark still lives. I am now bound to two. Super lovely.

Marasphyr beckons for me follow her and for Arias and Elias to remain. They don't look happy, but again, what the hell else can we do. She waves her hand, parting the water before the sword and we walk through the tunnel of waves. They close in on themselves as we pass, blocking the men from view. Now I'm completely alone with Marasphyr.

"I know what you are, Hunter," she says.

"Huh. It's actually Watcher now, so your knowledge is dated."

"I know the power you possess," she says, unaffected by my charming wit. "I can train you, Unseen Lord. Teach you the power of Shadow. Stay here, and you can master your abilities."

"I can't," I say, though I won't deny the pull. To learn what I can do, that would be something. I feel more growing in me, but I don't know how to tap into it. "I have people relying on me." A whole shit ton. Like all the people in the Nine freaking Worlds.

Marasphyr frowns, her eyes going distant. "I was once gifted with the power of sight. I have seen the future. If you leave, Unseen Lord, things will not end well."

Well, damn. That's not the kind of news a warrior likes to hear just before battle. "I have to try," I say.

"Very well," she says. "The choice has to be yours." She waves and the water around the sword disappears.

Something seems off about it though, now that it's not obscured by water. I peer more closely and shoot an accusing glance at Marasphyr. I grab the sword with two hands, pulling it from the light. "It's broken," I say, holding two pieces of one sword. "I thought the steel was indestructible."

Marasphyr shrugs.

"This is how it was before I came."

"What the hell am I supposed to do with a broken sword?" I ask, totally deflated.

"I told you I would give you the sword. I never told you it would be in one piece."

IRIS

e arrive back at the caves, broken sword in hand, feeling all kinds of pissed off. And the news gets worse from there.

Kayla pulls me aside. "I have some bad news," she says.

I raise an eyebrow at that. "More? I'm good. All full up on bad news today."

"The little girl you saved, Lala?"

My heart thumps hard against my ribs. "Yeah? What about her."

Don't say it. Don't freaking say it.

"I'm so sorry to tell you this, but she died a few minutes ago from injuries sustained during the storm."

She freaking said it. And everything in me burns. "Take me to her."

Without a word, Kayla walks through the cavern and down one of the paths that leads to smaller alcove. Elias follows us, his eyes shadowed. And there, before a fire, lay Lala, a blanket over her, her eyes closed, her face at peace, as her parents cry over her. When they see me, they beckon me in.

"You gave us more time with her," the mother says. "We will always be grateful for that."

"It wasn't enough," I choke out, as I drop to the ground next to the girl.

The fire burning in me is stoked by pain, by rage, by my own feelings of being let down. "I should be able to do something," I say through tears pouring down my face. "I'm the Unseen Lord. I can return from the dead, over and over. I should be able to do something!"

Elias puts a hand on my shoulder but it's Kayla who speaks. "Your brother had the power to bring others back. You have the power to bring yourself back. I'm so sorry."

"No. There's something more in me. I can feel it." I've been feeling it, for some time now I realize. Which is why it tempted me, for a moment, Marasphyr's offer. There is more I can learn. More I can do. And I don't know how to teach myself.

I place my hand over the child's heart, and I pour everything I have into her. My hand glows and that magic reaches into her body, lighting her up.

For a moment I feel hope. Can I do it? Can I bring her back from the dead?

I hold nothing back. Everything I am, all my power, all my belief, it all goes into her.

But what I call forth is not what I expect.

Her body does not rise, but a shadow of her does, her soul or spirit, perhaps.

She is luminous, glowing with my power, or maybe her own, as she smiles at me. "Thank you for the chance to say goodbye."

She turns to her parents, holding out her hands. They both sob and embrace her.

I would have thought with spirits, they would be intangible, but they are able to touch her, even as she hovers over her body. They speak in whispers, but I catch a few words. They are telling her of an afterlife where she will be loved and happy and safe and free. Where ancestors will guide her and look over her, where they themselves will join her one day.

I don't know what I believe about the afterlife. Never dying means never thinking of it. But I like to imagine that there's something out there. That we don't just cease to be. That feels a bit too depressing.

The girl turns to me at the end, as her spirit is fading, and touches my cheek. "You have everything you need," she says.

And then she is gone.

I leave the parents to grieve, hoping my unintentional act brought more healing than harm. Overcome with emotion I can't define, I escape down the winding caves until I am alone.

But Elias followed me. And relief floods me as he pulls me into his arms and lets me cry out everything building up in me.

I'm the most powerful Hunter in the worlds. The youngest Watcher. I don't cry.

But today. I cry. It is all too much to keep inside.

We stay that way for so long I lose track of time. My tears dry. My body folds into Elias's, a man I hunted for years. A man I haven't been able to stop thinking about. A man I might be falling in love with.

And then, the mood changes. The hug for comfort becomes something else. The fire of rage in me turns into a fire of need. Of desire.

There's so much death. Suffering. Pain. We are facing insurmountable odds. We might not survive. There's every possibility that I could die too many times in the war to come, and I will not come back. That Elias could die even once, and that would be the end.

But we are here now. Safe for now. Alone, for now. And I want him like I've never wanted anything.

My lips find his, and the kiss I pull from us both is filled with all the passion I've been keeping at bay. His strong arms tighten around me, his hand on my hips, fingers digging into me as I reach around his neck and pull him closer.

I feel his need growing, pushing against me, and I want to meet it. Want to take it all in. To feel something other than dire doom.

We are both still wet. Our clothes sticky and our attempt to release them clumsy, but it doesn't matter. We need this. When we are both naked, our bodies pressed against each other, we slow down, savoring the touch, the contact, the feeling. Against a stone wall, in a damp cave, everything else disappears.

My hands explore his chest, his abs, all of him, as his lips explore me, tracing lines of fire down my body, making promises as he goes.

The need rises, stoked by the movement of his hands, his tongue, his body. Until neither of us can resist anymore. He pushes me against the wall and lifts me onto his hips. We hold each other's eyes as he enters me, filling me, and then we are lost in each other.

The world seems to explode within us, a tide of magic pulling us into one. And when the need is satiated, and our bodies are spent, we stay connected, kissing, touching, memorizing each other. We may not have many more tomorrows, but we have tonight.

* * *

EVERYTHING HAS CHANGED and yet nothing has when we return to the cavern and to our friends who are waiting. If they know where we've been—what we've been doing—they give no indication. But Elias and I stand closer. Touch more often. Our bodies seem to be magnetically drawn together, even as we plan what to do next.

"I can fix the sword," Kayla says, resolving that problem. "I did make it, after all."

I like her confidence. And then an idea occurs to me. "I hate to sound like a diva, but… would it be possible to *not* make a sword? I mean, since it's already broken?"

Her lips twitch. "What did you have in mind?"

"I'm more of a dagger kinda girl, to be honest. Swords are so clunky. Daggers can get the job done like no other."

Arias smirks. "It's true. She has a special magic with those things. Especially when they're pointed at you."

"I can attest to that as well," Elias says.

"And yet you both live," Kayla says, raising an eyebrow.

Elias and Arias in unison steal my line. "She doesn't kill. Didn't anybody get the memo?"

I bust out laughing, and the guys look at each other sheepishly. Wow, this is awkward but also kinda hilarious and sweet.

"We need a forge," Kayla says. "And we need to reach the other princes. We'll need our own army if we're going to defeat the Tempest."

"Can we use a mirror to get to High Castle?" I ask. "It's likely the place the princes will try to secure once they realize their queen has gone mad. It has everything we need and proper defenses."

Tavian nods. "It's risky. She might already be there. But I think it's a risk worth taking."

"Right," Elias says, "but how do we get there?"

I smile sweetly at him. "You don't have any mirrors… hidden anywhere?"

"No, I do not."

"I'm guessing there's a story there," Arias says.

"Not one *you'll* ever hear," Elias retorts.

"Boys, boys. Play nice," I say to them both.

"We have a mirror hidden here," Kayla says. "We needed to be able to travel quickly. We can use that."

"Let's go then. Hey, where did Imenath go? He could be useful."

Kayla grins. "He's been a great help. Everyone, get supplies and let's meet at the cave entrance. I need to make sure someone here is in charge and taking care of everyone while we're gone."

Elias and I collect Theo and Duke, both of whom look not the least bit bothered at being left out of the recent adventures. They're warm, dry, and snuggling by a fire as Fae come forward, taking turns to pet and snuggle them. Spoiled boys!

"Think you can tear yourselves away from your fans?" I ask them.

Theo meows and pitter patters over to me, and I pick him up and tuck him in my shirt. Duke's way too big to tuck anywhere, so he just follows us. The pieces of the Midnight Sword are on my back in a canvas bag. That's about all we have.

"Ready?" I ask Elias.

He nods and we head to the cave entrance, where Kayla, Tavian, Arias, and Imenath await.

"Hey there buddy," I say, giving the big guy a pat on the arm. "Heard you've been super helpful."

Imenath smiles. "I will make good Hunter one day, yes?"

"We'll see. But I'm betting yes!"

His smile widens as Kayla leads us out of the cave and into the storm once again. She guides us around the mountain to another, smaller entrance that I would never have noticed had she not pointed it out. It's completely camouflaged. We slip in, wind down a few more corridors and end up facing a giant stone.

"Stand back," Kayla tells us, as Tavian steps forward.

He places his hands on the stone and they glow golden as he pushes the boulder, which must weigh a ton, to the side revealing a hidden nook with a mirror.

"Neat trick," I say.

He smiles. "Thanks."

Man of many words, that one.

Kayla touches the mirror. "Everyone, hold on." We do, and then we are pulled through the mirror and land in a dusty study surrounded by books.

"Welcome to High Castle," Kayla says, dusting her hands off on her pants.

"Let's see what's going on here," I say, opening the door in the study.

Two guards step forward, holding swords to my neck.

Okay then. Not the welcome I was hoping for, but here we are. "Who controls the castle?" I ask.

Elias is behind me about to go all killer vamp on their asses, but we need to make sure we aren't killing the good gals. (See what I did there?)

"Who's asking?" one of the guards asks.

"Wait? Is that… Iris the Watcher?" one asks.

"It is!" He peers behind me. "And Prince Elias. And Kayla Windhelm and Tavian Gray?"

They lower their swords and take off their helmets. "It's us. Roco and Marco!"

I grin. "Still guarding mirrors, I see."

"Oh no," Marco says. At least, I think he's Marco. "We were forgiven and now we're guarding the castle."

"The mirror in the castle," I point out.

They both frown.

"But yes, the castle. That's a big job. Well done!" I pat them each on the shoulder.

That cheers them up.

"Who's in charge here?" I ask, crossing my fingers and praying to all the gods it's not Aya.

"Well, Prince Asher gives the most orders, but Prince Zeb says he's no more in charge than any of them. Prince Ace doesn't say much, but did blow up a room, and Prince Dean has been locked in the library studying," Roco says.

"This is excellent news," Elias says. "Take us to my uncle."

They look at each other. "Which one?"

"Asher," he says.

They look a little worried, but they do as ordered.

We meander through corridors and halls that all kinda look the same if I'm being totally honest. Until we finally reach the throne room. Asher is sitting on the throne arguing with Zeb, who's kind of perched on the throne next to him but not really? Like he wants to sit down, but isn't quite sure?

The guards surrounding them come to attention when they see us, but Asher rises, waving them away. "It's good to see you all. Now can someone tell me what the bloody hell you did to our queen?."

"That's a bit of a story," I say. "How about some dry clothes, food, wine and a fire and we'll tell you all about it?"

He looks at the sagging mess we are and nods, calling for a servant. "Prepare quarters for all of them, baths, meals, clothes and then find all the princes and tell them to meet in the war room."

The servant nods and gestures for us to follow her.

I won't bore you with all these details. It's pretty basic. Elias and I get a room together, that's the most exciting part. And I'm pretty stoked at the idea of sleeping with him tonight, if I'm being totally honest, and not just because I'm utterly exhausted.

We bathe, change, eat, all the things, and once we are feeling mostly ourselves, we join the princes and tell the whole story again of what happened and all about the secret

Storm Spirit—as an aside, boy was Asher super not happy to find out secrets were kept that he wasn't in on.

When we were done, they all looked thoughtful. "So you can repair the sword?" Asher asks.

"Yes," Kayla says.

"And you have the bow?" he looks at Arias, his expression puzzled.

"Yes, in my quarters," Arias says.

Elias is bitter about that. He thinks we should hold onto it.

"But no one has any idea about the mantle?" Zeb asks, looking at Dean.

Dean shakes his head. "I've heard of it, of course, but no word at all where it could be, and I haven't come across any news in my reading."

Fun fact about Dean. He's freaking gorgeous, and I def feel the pull that he has, but I'm pretty smitten with his nephew, so that's a hard no. The dude exudes sexiness though, and it's quite a shock to realize how bloody brilliant he is. He's probably the most well-read of all the princes, which is stunning, really, for a man who has an aversion to wearing shirts, like right now for instance. Come on, dude, cover up those nippers will ya?

"We have other ways of fighting her," Ace says. "But..." his eyes are pained. "Is there no other way? She's our niece. Our queen. Ari and Fen's daughter. I..."

This is clearly tearing him up. They are close, it's clear. But. "Have you seen the storms ravaging the kingdom?" I ask.

They all nod.

"It will only get worse," Arias says. "It will tear Inferna and Avakiri apart, and then it will move on."

"She's already ripped a hole in the fabric or the universe, or some shit," I say. "This is gonna get bad real fast, guys. We have to stop her."

"Why would she do this?" Ace asks, planting his face in the palm of his hand. "She was queen. She was loved. She was strong and powerful. Why?"

"She was jealous," I say. "Of her parents, for their power. And she felt they were ruling the kingdom with weakness. I think her initial intentions were good, but from what I've heard and seen, it's not just her in there anymore."

"Did you see her Spirit?" Ace asks.

"No. It hadn't manifested yet," I say.

"Legends say it is a Thunder Bird," Arias says. "She will have the power of flight, and it will be powerful."

Wonderful. "Well, I've got Theo."

Varis nods. "And I have my Air Spirit, plus Kayla has her Fire Spirit."

"Good," I say. "So we've got some air potential. She'll likely come for the castle. What has she been doing so far?"

Asher frowns. "Destroying the Outlands. From what we've been told they are ravaged. Hundreds dead."

Oh damn. That's not good.

"What's happening to your people while you are all here?" I ask.

"Each of our Realms has safe holds our people have been led into. They won't last, but it's the best we can do until we stop her."

"Okay, so now we need a plan to stop her," I say. "Using just two of the Shadow's Bane, and whatever magic, cleverness and skill we each possess in this room."

"I have ideas," Ace says. "Some inventions that can be useful."

"And Varis and I have power we can use to help create shields and improve offensive maneuvers," Tavian says.

"Let's get to it then."

* * *

WE ALL WORK well into the night, and there is still much to do, but we also recognize we need our rest for what's to come. We don't know when she'll strike, we just know she will. She wants her base of power back. I know that for certain.

When Elias and I crawl into bed, with Theo and Duke at our feet, it isn't for more romance, but the gentle companionship of his arms around me as I collapse into exhaustion is its own kind of comfort.

For the next several days, this routine repeats. We all pitch in, preparing the defenses of the castle, making sure the guards are armed and ready, making sure everyone has a job and is doing it.

And through it all we get birds coming in with messages from the other Realms. Messages of destruction. Death. Chaos. The storm is worsening. The castle is taking a beating. But we are near water, where Arias's powers are strongest. And we have defenses. If we go out to find her, we lose all advantage and become more vulnerable, and more likely to lose. Already the odds are not great.

The night the storm comes for us, I am lying in bed, head on Elias's chest, listening to the howling rain outside, when lightning cracks through the window, setting our bed on fire.

We jump out and dress quickly, sending Duke and Theo out to alert the others.

"She's here," I say, though, duh, that's pretty obvious.

Time to party.

IRIS

The sun rises over the mountains. Golden rays fall across the valley and rivers of Inferna, only to be dimmed by the gathering storm on the horizon. Thunder crashes in the distance. Lightning scars the sky.

I stand on the edge of a watchtower overlooking the land below, waiting for my new daggers to be completed, my black cloak and leather armor soaking in the growing rain which chatters like teeth around me. A massive army has formed off the shores of the lake surrounding the castle. Vampires loyal to Queen Aya. And they look ready to devour.

Our own army is small in comparison. A string of pebbles attempting to withstand a mighty wave. Some are too young to fight. Some too old. Some piss themselves at the sight of our foe. I am glad the Prince of Darkness will fight at my side, though at the moment Elias is away, checking on the craftsmanship of Kayla and Ace. However, his brother, the water druid, is here.

Arias hands me the Twilight Bow and I sling it over my shoulder. The ancient weapon glows silver in the dimming light, illuminating my surroundings, making me seem like some ethereal ghost amidst the darkness. I flex my hands, steeling myself for the battle to come.

A beast of lightning and thunder tears through the sky, screeching a terrible sound. A Thunder Bird. The spirit manifested in physical form. Its large, about the size of a full grown manticore, with large wings of silver and blue feathers that ripple with sparks. Its eyes are lightning bolts that sizzle in its hawk like head. It is a predator. A being of chaos. And it has come to end us all.

The Tempest sits atop her new spirit, clad in feathered armor so she looks an extension of the bird itself. Her black cape trails behind her, billowing in the brisk harsh wind. Her silver hair drifts erratically through the air. Her eyes are cold.

"Nice outfit," I scream over the thunder. "Did your pet there donate some feathers for it? It is twinsies day? I must not have gotten the memo!"

The Tempest—and I say the Tempest because I'm having a hard time seeing anything of Aya left—laughs. "You always have had a lovely wit, Iris. It will be a shame to remove that from the world. Yield the castle, hand over the bow, and cease your stand against me, and I may yet let you live."

I pause as if considering. "Tempting. Super tempting. But I'm gonna have to say, nah, Sis. Can't do it."

"Then we war! And you will all die!"

"Right, yeah, or... " I stroke my chin. "You know, this weather is really shit for that kind of thing. How about we duke it out over chess? Best of three games wins?"

The Tempest, hovering in the middle of her storm, does not look amused.

"No chess? What about a scavenger hunt? Or a dance battle?" I pause, waiting for her response.

"Nothing? Wow, tough crowd." I know I'm going to lose her soon, but I need my blades. Hurry up, Elias and Kayla.

We're out of time. "A few more ideas, just to toss out there. Cook off? Best Rube Goldberg machine?"

"Best... what?" Now she looks confused and pissed. Awesome.

"Rube Goldberg machine? You know, a machine that takes something super simple and deliberately makes it waaay more complicated than it should be? That's right up your alley, right? What with this really round about way you're trying to... I don't even know what you're trying to do anymore. Do you? Cuz the Aya I knew wanted peace. Maybe she wanted it in a way I didn't agree with, but that was the end goal. This—" I gesture to her super nova form with her crazy bird. "This isn't the Aya I knew. And destroying the worlds and everyone in them isn't gonna get you shit, my friend. Sorry to be the one to tell you."

She cocks her head. "You're stalling."

I smile and raise my bow. "Yeah, but took you long enough to figure it out." And I unleash a flurry of arrows into her and the bird.

Lightning flashes around them and the arrows burst into flames, falling from the sky. Well, shit. That didn't go how I'd hoped.

She soars into the sky, roaring, holding her hands up, calling forth all the fury of the storm, and directs it into the center of the castle.

That's Ace's cue. He unleashes special lightning rod projectiles with trimantium cores to attract the lightning and catch it, in a manner of speaking. I don't know the ins and outs, that's his department.

It works reasonably well. Some of the lightning is diverted, but the castle still takes heavy damage, and I can hear people screaming. I cringe.

"You bitch," I holler, throwing my fury at her. "Do you know what you did to that village on the island? You killed a little girl named Lala who had the sweetest smile and parents who loved her. Is that your idea of peace?"

"I've realized peace can only be had when you remove the elements of discord. In this case, that would be people."

"Well, that's going to get lonely pretty damn fast," I say, loosing another series of arrows.

While we fight, Arias uses his power to channel the waters of the moat around the castle, creating walls with them, moving them over land as his serpent appears in them and attacks her from behind. This has the bonus affect of taking out some of her ground army, who are storming the castle. The wall of water slams into her and the serpent coils around the bird, but with a flick of her wrist, she pulls her cape around her and blinks away, into shadows, taking her bird with her and appearing to the right, away from the serpent.

And then I get it. I finally get it.

We've had the Shadow's Mantle all along.

Aya has been wearing it.

With perfect timing, Elias and Kayla run up, and she presents me my daggers. "Ace helped me. Sorry it took so long but we added a special touch to them."

"Cool, thanks. Gotta go. I'm about to retrieve the third piece of the Shadow's Bane."

With that, I stick the daggers into their sheaths, swing the bow around my back and hop onto Theo. "Distract her for me," I say, as we take to the air.

At this point, a lot happens. After regrouping, Arias gets his Spirit in on the action once again. Kayla fires up her Phoenix (see what I did there? Fire Spirit... fires up? Even in battle I'm that good) and sets it to attack mode on the Thunder Bird. Varis and Tavian both use their mojo to help protect the castle and save the people in the cross fires.

We armed the soldiers with wooden bows rather than

swords, since the metal would just electrify them, but mostly it's going to be up to us to stop her.

I face off with her, mid-air, pulling out a dagger and flipping it in my palm. Oh, this is nice. Perfect balance, firm grip, beautiful design. I hope I don't lose these, because I'm seriously in love.

"Hey, Aya. I like your cloak."

She looks up, surprised, and I let my dagger lose.

My aim is impeccable. I even account for her attempt to blink away. But I'm really, really fast, especially with my power pulsing through me like fire. The dagger hits the clasp on her cloak, breaking it. And then, my dagger flies back to my palm. That's amazing. I'm going to kiss Kayla—and Ace—when this is over. The black fabric falls off her shoulders, and before she even realizes what's going on, Theo takes us to it. I snatch it out of the air and secure it around my neck. And then I feel it.

The power of the Shadow's Bane.

But it's not necessarily a new power. It's an old power that always lived in me, and the magic in these artifacts awakens it.

Using my daggers once again, I throw them simultaneously, one at her throat, the other at her bird. Together, they fall from the sky, and as my daggers return to me, I unleash a flurry of arrows on them, then dash down with Theo to land on the ground next to them.

They are both bleeding, lightning pouring out of their wounds, but it hasn't slowed them much.

And her power is growing. The storm is increasing in intensity. Lightning breaks apart the earth, splitting it in two, and cracking open a wall in the castle. Guards fall to their death screaming. Rage boils in me.

Her soldiers attack, pouring into the castle.

My people need backup. We're overpowered.

My friends are using everything they can to defend the castle and the people in it, but it's not enough.

And with all the power I have, I explode.

The sun darkens as the moon rises prematurely covering it.

The earth trembles, and it's not from the storm.

I have become the storm.

The Tempest lashes at me with her lightning, but I dodge it, blinking into the shadows.

Something big. Something powerful awakens in me and I hold out my hands and call for help.

And from around the world, the dead awaken, their Spirits called forth in masses, and they arrive on the beach of High Castle to kill their enemies.

IRIS

$\mathcal{C}$haos abounds. I don't even know how I did what I did, and I really hope there are no negative side effects. Like, I didn't read the fine print on all this, you know?

But at least our soldiers have some back up while I face the Tempest, who is still in full on rage mode.

She mounts her Thunder Bird and takes to the sky, and Theo and I follow, unleashing arrows and daggers—and damn do I love these things—hoping to slow her.

She is glowing. Completely consumed. Ready to rip apart everything in her path.

"Aya. Stop! You must still be in there somewhere. Stop!"

She doesn't hear me—or ignores me—I don't know which. This isn't working. How do I kill her? Even with all this, with my powers and the Shadow's Bane, it seems impossible. The Spirit is too strong. Too wild.

I have an idea. I dive Theo towards the castle and call for Ace. "It's Plan B time," I tell him. "This is so freaking risky," I say, as he climbs onto Theo behind me. "Are you sure about this?"

The handsome genius nods. "Maybe I can reach her. If anyone can."

We take to the skies again, and lest you've forgotten, let me remind you it's still pouring rain. So much rain. O.M.G. I'm done with this. Completely done.

When we are close enough to Aya for her to hear us, Ace makes his plea.

"Aya, you can fight this Spirit. You can stop its path of destruction. I know you can. You're the strongest, bravest person I've ever know."

"I am not the girl you knew, Uncle. I am so much more. Stand aside, so you do not fall. You can help raise a new world, a new people, without the chaos, without the fighting, without the pain."

"That's impossible," he says. "Life is pain. But pain is just a feeling. A fleeting, temporary experience that doesn't have to create suffering. Not if you don't let it."

She releases the lightning held in her hands and scorches the earth below us, tearing more bits of the castle apart, killing more innocent people.

Ace sighs. He knows what he must do, but I can only imagine how hard it is for him to do it.

He opens his cloak and pulls out a special arrow, tipped with trimantium, and gives it to me.

"I'm sorry, dear girl. You'll always be in my heart."

I knock and loose the arrow straight at her heart.

Without the cloak, she can't blink out.

It strikes her and she screams, her lightning surging into her, pulling out of the sky. It looks like it's working, like we'll actually defeat her.

But then she smiles and rips the arrow out of her chest. "You think this can stop me now? Nothing can contain what I've become."

And she shoots us out of the sky with lightning. It vibrates inside my body, and for the second time, the Storm Spirit kills me, taking Ace and Theo down too.

I Renew on shore and jog to Ace and Theo. My Manticore roars, shaking, and hobbles next to me. I run a hand over him to make sure he's not injured and check on Ace, but he's not breathing.

"You killed him!" I scream into the sky. "Your favorite uncle, the man who taught you everything. You killed him. And for what?"

Aya lands beside us, and I pull out my daggers. I don't have any lives left. This is it. If she kills me again, I'm dead too.

Her power fades a fraction as she stares at the body of her uncle. I can see her eyes flicker, her natural color returning in flashes, as if the old Aya is fighting back. She drops to her knees. "Uncle Ace?"

"He's gone," I say.

"No. This isn't what I meant to do. This isn't how I wanted it to end. I just wanted to help. To make things right. To make the world safe."

I look around with a sardonic laugh. "How's that working for you?"

She turns on me and pulls out a sword filled with electricity, her Thunder Bird at her side, ready to lunge at me. I'm ready. Mostly. I got this.

But then she twists to the side and plunges her sword into the bird's heart, screaming as she does, as a hole appears in her chest, as lightning pours out. "I'm sorry!" she cries.

An explosion of light distorts the air around us, and the lightning pulses, forming into a ball.

I can feel it seeking. Looking for somewhere to go.

Looking for someone to channel its power.

I back away, sweat pooling on my face and under my arms. Shit. Shit. Shit. Shit.

And as the ball races towards me, ready to consume me, Theo throws himself in its path, taking the hit right in the chest as he falls to the sand, lifeless.

*　*　*

EVERYTHING PAUSES. The world seems to go mute. Rain stops. Lightning ceases. The clang of battle disappears. The sun returns.

Am I dreaming? Am I dead? For real dead?

At my feet, my brave Manticore lays there unmoving, and I drop my body over his, crying, begging him to come back to me.

The spirits I called from the dead have disappeared, and I search myself for a spark that will let me bring him back. I pour a piece of myself into him, giving him part of me.

There's a zing under my hands.

A tiny zap of lightning.

And Theo awakens.

His fur turning brighter silver.

His eyes glow with lightning.

But when he meows and pushes his big head against my hand, I know he's still my Theo.

I crawl over to Ace and check him, then pull out the vial he gave me earlier and administer it. It takes a moment, and I worry the lightning ruined this plan, but he sputters and sits up, looking around. "Did it work?" he asks.

"It did. Thinking she had killed you brought her back to herself, just as we'd hoped. She fought the Spirit. It entered Theo, but he seems okay."

Ace turns quizzically towards my Manticore, studying

him. "Interesting. Theo's magic must be a stabilizer for the Storm Spirit. I've never seen such a thing. How fascinating."

I help Ace up and we look for Aya, or her body, but she's nowhere to be found. "What do you think happened to her?" I ask him.

He shrugs. "She should pay for her crimes. But to be honest, I hope she escaped. I hope she has learned from this. And I hope she finds a way to be at peace within herself."

We mount Theo and fly to the castle. I seek out Elias first, and seeing him alive and well, something breaks in me and I throw myself at him, crying. Arias, Kayla, Tavian, Varis, Asher, Dean and Zeb all came out fine. But hundreds more didn't. There are many bodies to burn. Many lives to mourn.

Imenath struts out from the shadows, his face aglow. "I have saved the castle," he says.

I laugh. "Well done, buddy. I'll put in a good word for you with the Council."

And then I turn to Elias. "We have to go check on your mother. This should have broken the curse."

Leaving the others to clean up the mess—or at least start to, as this will be a very long process— we head back to the island, where the people have already begun to reclaim their home from the devastation. It will take a long time to rebuild, and I make a mental note to make sure they are sent whatever they need to make the process easier.

We find Ari in the caves, still chained. But her eyes have cleared.

When she sees us, she cries. "I'm so sorry. For everything."

Elias rushes to her and unlocks her bounds, and they hug for a long time. We get her back to High Castle where healers work with her to restore her mind and health.

There is much to be done to fix the damage Aya caused, but in a way this has brought the kingdoms of Inferna and

Avakiri together. They were all affected, and Aya was of both bloods. They must rebuild together.

Elias and I hold hands as we stand on the shores of High Castle. Theo and Duke stand beside us. It's been a long week, and more long weeks to come, but finally, the sun is shining, and it is a warm, beautiful day.

Dum Spiro Spero.

While I breathe, I hope.

EPILOGUE: IRIS

he sun is high in the sky and I'm soaking in all the rays as I lay on the grass outside my house, my head resting on my llama, Wit. It's a rare moment of not doing anything significant. Just picking out images in the clouds and daydreaming.

"Don't you have a date to get to?" Uncle Sly asks as he approaches from the house, long purple robes dragging in the dirt. Dude does not go outside much and it shows. He's really more of an indoor kinda guy. It's almost comical seeing him out and about on such a glorious day.

I stretch and raise myself, giving my llamas one more kiss on the head each.

"I have plenty of time. Besides, I needed some recovery after that shit show of a Council meeting," I say with a grin.

"Expect plenty more like those, my dear. Welcome to life on the Council."

That's right, you heard him. Your girl, Iris, isn't just a Watcher anymore. I'm officially representing the vampires on the Council. Apparently being Unseen Lord makes me enough vampire to fill that role, now that Thalius has been demoted.

But man-oh-man, there's a whole shit ton of mess to clean up. Thalius had his ass kicked back down to Hunter, and let me tell you he's a pain in the ass to deal with. Turns out he wasn't corrupt, just incompetent and blind with ambition.

And guess who took over Aya's spot? The man of the hour, my sweetheart, Elias Vane Spero, who is no longer on the Most Wanted List. All charges were dropped once the truth came out about the Tempest and Lix Tetrax and all that shadowy nonsense. That whole group has been infiltrated. Baddies identified. Those in against their will exonerated. It's time to clean up the Hunter's Council from the inside and make it what it should be.

"How's Imenath taking to his Hunter-in-Training status?" I ask. I'm proud of the little guy. He's really made something of himself. And I wasn't the only one impressed, which is why it was agreed he'd paid back his debt to society—after all he'd risked his life in the recent war—and could now train to be a Hunter.

Uncle Sly chuckles. "He's doing as one might imagine. A lot of boisterous gloating without a lot of skill to back it up, but he has potential. He'll get there."

I grin at that news. It's just as I expected. "Any news from Callie?" She's once again disappeared, still seeking the truth, whatever that means, but I get letters from her occasionally. As if on cue, Uncle Sly pulls a parchment from his robes, and I grin and take it, slipping it into the pocket of my jeans.

Don't judge, it's casual Friday.

Uncle Sly slips an arm over my shoulder as we walk back to my house. "I'm proud of you, Iris. I always have been, and I'm especially proud now. You've saved the worlds, and you've grown as a person."

"How so?" I ask as we approach my door.

"You always saw things in black and white. Good versus evil. Which is all well and fine, and served you as a Hunter. But as a Council Member, being able to see the nuances is incredibly important. Your relationship with Elias and his brother, and even with Aya, have helped you see that most of life is shades of gray, and we must use careful judgement and wise discernment to gauge the proper path. It's not as easy, but it's necessary and more truthful."

"You're not wrong, Uncle, though I confess I still sometimes long for the days when everything seemed more simple."

"You saw things as a child then. Now, you see things as an adult. But I understand the appeal. Childhood is simple, for most. Adulthood is a complex web. I have been the latter too long to even remember what the former feels like. Raising you and Callie actually helped me to recapture that sense of youth. You two were good for me, even if I wasn't always the best for you," he says, a touch of unexpected melancholy in his voice.

I turn to him and pull him into a hug. "You were exactly what I needed. Who else could have raised the Unseen Lord and one of the most powerful succubi in the all the Nine Worlds? And look how great we turned out," I tease, pulling back.

He wipes his eyes, and I swear I see a tear, but that can't be. Uncle Sly never cries.

He covers his emotions with a smile. "I took the liberty of having something new made for your date tonight. I encourage you to wear it."

I raise an eyebrow at that. "Really? Dressing me for my dates now? This is different. Did Callie put you up to this?"

He chuckles. "No, just me being a sentimental old fool.

Now go get changed and hop over to Inferna. You have a prince waiting."

With a kiss on the cheek, he leaves me to it, and I wander through the living room, with only a short longing glance at my gaming station—I haven't had time to play a proper marathon in ages—and head to my bedroom.

Hanging from a mannequin—which wasn't there before, just FYI—is a stunning pale cream gown trimmed with fur and pearl. It has a plunging neckline and form fitting waist that flares from the hips. It's truly the most beautiful gown I've ever seen. I have no idea why Uncle Sly thinks I need to be this dressed up. I don't usually get this fancy for dates with Elias, of which, thank the gods, we've had many! But I can't refuse such a gift, so after a shower and quick dry of my hair, I slip into it, donning the matching shoes as the final touch. Once my hair and makeup are done, I assess myself in the mirror. Yup—I can still see myself, and I can travel through them. I guess being the most badass vampire has its perks. Not to mention I don't need to live off blood. Another huge perk.

Elias installed a secret mirror in his castle so that he and I can get to each other in mere moments.

I touch my mirror, think of him, and step through.

On the other side, Elias is there, waiting for me. He's dressed to the nines, as they say, and looking far too handsome than any man has any right to. And he's holding a bouquet of wild flowers—my favorite.

No words are spoken as he pulls me into his arms. The feeling of his touch, of being close to him, of his smell... it feels like being home and I never want to leave. After a time I look up at him and he grins, then leans in to kiss me. We've kissed a lot, I won't lie. Like, a ton, since the whole almost end of the worlds shenanigans, and it never gets old. As always, it lights a fire in me that will have to wait until later.

He pulls back, his eyes, luminous. "I have a surprise for you," he says, holding my hand and guiding me out of the secret room and into his castle. It's still going through renovations after years of neglect, but it's finally looking respectable. It's built of white stone glistening with crystal and is now decked out with new furniture, rugs, proper lighting, hearths to keep the chill at bay, and a staff that helps everything run smoothly. And Prince Elias has taken to his position with skill and wisdom, just as I knew he would.

The sun is setting in Inferna, and Elias takes me to the shores of his kingdom, where a small boat awaits. Magical flying balls of light guide our way and once we are settled onto the pillows, with goblets of wine and platters of food for us to enjoy, the boat winds down the waters taking us wherever Elias has planned.

"So, where is this mystery date?" I ask.

"You'll see. Be patient, my love. We're almost there."

You heard right, little bird. I'm his love. I know, it gets me in the feels too. But after all these months, everything is finally turning out the way it was meant to all along. I can't imagine anything more perfect.

The boat slows and we arrive at a clearing that has a table set for two, with candles, delicious food, and a field of glowing flowers surrounding us. Thousands of them. It's the most spectacular sight I've ever seen.

He escorts me to my chair and takes his. From somewhere beyond my vision, a soft melody emerges from the woods around us. The music is haunting and the setting is beyond magical. "What is this place?" I ask.

"This is the rare and coveted woodlands of the fairies. Different than the Fae, the fairies are small creatures who only show themselves when they want to, and that isn't often. I didn't even realize until recently that my kingdom boasts one of the only woodlands left on Inferna. The few others that remain are in Avakiri."

"It's astonishing," I say. "And the music?"

"The fairies themselves," he says with a wink.

Before us are plates of food, savory and delicious. We eat and talk. I fill him in on all that's happening in my life, and the latest from Callie, he tells me about the challenges and treasures of being prince of his realm. We talk about the Council a bit, and what we want to see happen there. We can't help it. It's work, yes, and totally not romantic, but it's important to both of us.

After dinner and a delightful strawberry treat for dessert, courtesy of his Uncle Zeb, Elias takes a small box from his pocket.

You know the kind of box I'm talking about.

One of *those* boxes.

And my heart stops. Then skips. Then stops again.

And Elias smiles, like he knows what I'm thinking cuz I totally know what he's doing.

He gets down on one knee.

Opens the box.

And there's a spider inside!

Just kidding. Had you fooled.

Of course there's not a spider in there. He would never do that to me.

What do you think is in the little black velvet box?

A big ass diamond ring of course!

"Iris," he says, his voice ringing in the air like bells. I don't even know what that means, but that's how it feels okay? Like bells. "You have been the unexpected missing piece in my life, one I didn't know I needed until I found you. I know we live in different worlds, literally, and that I'm asking a lot as prince of a realm in Inferna, but—"

"Yes!" I say, unable to contain myself.

"But I wasn't finished," he says, teasingly.

"The answer is still yes. Do you want to finish though. You can. Go ahead."

He stands and pulls me to him. "The speech can wait." He slips the ring on my finger and we kiss under the stars, in a field of glowing flowers, as fairies come out of hiding to dance and sing around us.

To say it was the most magical proposal to ever happen would be an understatement.

We rush back to the castle as fast as we can and retire to his quarters. Duke is there waiting for us, with Theo. Neither of them were happy to be left out, but we give both some hugs and kisses and tell them the news. Then we kick them off the bed and tell them to stay clear for a few hours.

Elias's hands send shivers up my spine as he gently removes my dress. I help him with his waste coat and buttons and once we are both in our birthday suits we slip into his bed, our bodies pressing close as we explore every inch of each other.

This will never get old. Being with him. Touching him. Loving him.

It will never get old, even when we do.

* * *

THE NEXT MORNING WE DRESS, eat, and with Duke and Theo in tow, make our way to High Castle to tell the queen and Elias's uncles—who have been notified to meet us there--the good news.

Queen Arianna has resumed her seat on the throne, and her kingdom couldn't be happier. But there's still a deep sadness in her eyes.

When we arrive she is in the Great Hall sipping tea, her

dragon perched on her shoulder. Dean sits next to her, with Asher across from her. Zeb is reading a book and sipping at his goblet, but looks up to say hi when we approach. Ace paces in front of the fire, lost in his own thoughts. He hasn't been the same since the war with Aya. He misses her, that's clear. And feels betrayed too, I think. There's an empty spot in everyone's heart over Aya, and the path her life took, and King Fenris, whose whereabouts is still unknown.

Ari rises to greet us, smiling as she does. She and I have grown close since our time in the caves, and I consider her a dear friend now. Healers have been working with her to mend the damage the curse did on her mind, but I fear the real damage is to her heart. She misses her daughter and husband. "Any news on Fen?" I ask.

Her eyes alight. "There might be," she says with an optimism I haven't seen in her before.

Dean stands, kisses my cheek and shakes Elias's hand and grins. "I've had news of an artifact on earth... a piece of the Fallen Star of Nirandel. It's just rumor, but word is, Fen is somehow connected to this. That's all I know, but I leave in the morning to investigate."

"What's your first step?" Elias asks, as anxious about his father as anyone.

"My sources tell me there's a renowned archaeologist who's apparently on the hunt for it. An... Alex Stone. I'm going to find him and see what he knows, take it from there."

Ari squeezes his hand. They have always been close, though for many years Dean wanted more. Now he seems content with her as a friend and sister. "Many don't realize that Dean has a PhD in Archeology, and is renowned on Earth himself," she says with sisterly pride. "It's good to see you putting your skills to work. Keep me informed, will you?"

He kisses her forehead with affection. "Of course. You'll

be the first person to know what I discover. We will find Fen. He's out there somewhere."

The pain is her eyes breaks my heart as she nods. "I know you will."

The heartfelt moment is broken by a choir of young voices echoing around us as the wind begins to howl. And the song they sing is thus...

He'll come in the night
In armor of white
Riding a steed of snow

Three signs there are
That mean he's not far
Silver army in tow

First comes the frost
Second the flame
Third are the voices
of those he has slain

THUD.

Thud.

Thud.

Footsteps. They come from the darkness. Drawing near.

Thud.

Thud.

Thud.

The sound of hooves clacking on icy stone.

And then I see him.

The White Rider.

"Arias, stop that nonsense," Ari says, laughing.

Arias walks across the room and grins. "Sorry, couldn't help it. Old habits and all."

He kisses his mother then kisses my cheek and shakes Elias's hands. He and Elias aren't quite buddy-buddy yet, but they're working on it. Kayla and Tavian follow him in. "Everyone's here now. What's the big news?" he asks.

I hold up my hand to show off my new ring, and there's laughter and cheers and hugs from everyone.

Arias pulls me aside and smiles. "I'm truly happy for you both. I'm glad things have worked out."

"Me too," I say.

For the rest of the day we feast and celebrate. Someone gets word to Uncle Sly, and in a rare departure from his standard protocol, he joins us at High Castle. I've got my whole family together. Well, everyone except Callie, but wherever she is, I know she'd be happy for me.

We don't have answers to questions about dates and logistics. Where will we live? I don't know. Could we maybe take turns living at each other's places? When's the big day? No clue. These questions can wait.

Today is about enjoying the moment and celebrating the love we have for each other and our family.

Tomorrow we can figure the rest out.

THE END

Ready for the next adventure? Get Vampire Girl: Fallen Star on Amazon!

Vampire Girl 7: Fallen Star

SNEAK PEEK: FALLEN STAR

 ou may be wondering what a girl like me is doing in a place like this. Dark. Damp. Filled with mummified corpses too old to name. Creepy crawlies that you don't even want to know about. *Crunch* Ew. I think I just crushed one with my palm.

Give me a sec while I wipe the goo off my hands.

Even the dust smells like it's lived and died a thousand times since the last human stepped foot in here.

And yet here I am, cobwebs in my hair, bug goo oozing into the cracks of my fingers despite my best effort to rub the crap off on the stone, crawling on my hands and knees through a narrow tunnel that should lead me to a cavern.

'Should' being the operative word here.

Well, let me set the record straight. First, I'm not a girl, I'm a woman. Notice the date on my driver's license? Fully fledged grown-up. Also, those two PhDs at the end of my name are hard to come by as a girl. Factor in that I got my degrees by the age of twenty-five, and you can perhaps understand why I don't like being called girl. I graduated high school at sixteen. College at eighteen. Two PhDs in six years seemed a bit behind the curve, to be honest. I'm still bummed about that.

But life is full of little disappointments, isn't it?

The question is, will this tomb be a disappointment as well, or will we finally find what we've been scouring the world for?

"See anything, Alex?" Trevor's voice startles a critter near my foot, who makes a dash for my legs and tries to shimmy up my pants. Jokes on him, though. I learned long ago to keep that shit tucked in tight. That was a life lesson best not repeated. I still have the scars as a reminder.

Not finding a way in, the little beast screeches and scurries away. Probably to tell his friends all about the two delicious morsels waiting in the wings.

Trevor and I being those morsels, in case that was unclear.

"Nothing yet," I answer, trying to keep my voice low so as not to disturb whatever else might be living here.

While my partner might not believe anything that science can't definitively prove, I've seen enough to know we don't know everything. In fact, we don't know much at all. And not to toot my own horn, but I know a whole hell of a lot, so that's saying something.

Trevor's never been on an excavation like this before. He has no clue that's the real reason his company hired me. He thinks I'm here to fulfill some kind of PC vagina quota. That we're just searching for a rare artifact worth a lot of money. Something that museum's worldwide will drool over. Something that will unlock a few more secrets of the past.

Nothing wrong with that (err..., except for the vagina quota bullshit. I refer you back to my double PhDs). For the rest, well, we've all got to start somewhere.

But, I know better.

I know what we seek holds power. Real power.

Power I can't let Global Tech get their hands on. Which is the only reason I took this gig. To double-cross them.

I know, not very sportsmanlike. But if you knew what was at stake, you'd do the same. Trust me.

Plus, they're not the only ones after it. Dr. Vane's team—an archaeologist of questionable repute who has beaten me to more than a few precious finds—is en route as we speak, according to sources who know shit. I can't let that old man get his hands on this. Way too dangerous for someone with ties to not-quite-legal organizations who are known to smuggle rare artifacts into other countries and sell them to private collectors on the black market. If I ever meet the greedy son of a bitch in person, I have a few choice words to share with him. But, alas, he keeps a low profile.

I do too, but not for nefarious reasons. I do it mostly for my reputation. As young as I am, I look even younger. I'm working at reaching 5'5", but can only manage with heels, I'm compact—or what some would call 'scrappy' and my short pale blonde hair usually features a few fun colors. I get carded a lot. My look doesn't help instill respect and clout in a middle-aged white dude's club. So, I stay off social media, keep my pictures out of newspapers and online write-ups, and let my work speak for itself. Most people mistake me for a middle-aged white dude. Imagine their surprise!

I squint as the darkness that edges around the thin beam of light from my headlamp begins to brighten, and I feel a shift in the air around me. "We're coming up to something," I say.

Trevor grunts in response, and a few more critters frolic around our hands. Something bites the thick part of my palm, and I hold back a curse and smash the bastard against the stone, feeling it's small bones break. I can't move my head enough to look at my hand, but I feel blood pooling. I'll have to get something on that soon. Who knows what kind of infections these creatures carry.

I slow my pace, knowing I could be crawling into a trap. And then I stop completely and suddenly, my heart a drum against my ribs. Trevor bumps into me.

"What's the holdup?"

I look down, and my light doesn't carry far. If I'd kept going, I would have crawled off the edge into total darkness. "We've got a bit of a problem," I tell him. "But I have a plan."

It's not a great plan. But it's a plan. I explain it, and though I can't see his face, I know the look he's giving me.

He didn't like giving up control of this excavation to a 'girl.' He was also expecting a dude. But we worked it out. And in the course of things somehow ended up in bed.

Probably a mistake. But a fun one, I will admit. I'd like to say it had nothing to do with his sculpted body, dark bedroom eyes and wicked grin, but I'd be lying. I'm still a woman, after all. I have needs.

And in a job like mine, I take the fun where it can be had.

Still, our roll in the hay didn't erase the sharp edges of misogyny embedded in Trevor's DNA. So this plan isn't an easy sell.

Fortunately, I don't need his permission. He can join, or stay on his hands and knees and wait for me to discover the artifact and claim the credit. You want to bet he'll stay and wait?

Didn't think so.

I pull out two climbing picks and prepare for the crazy part. This is where it gets tricky, because I have very little room to maneuver, I don't know what's below us, and all manner of shit could hit the proverbial fan.

In one fluid movement, I slam the picks into the rock, launch myself out of the shaft I'd been crawling through, and spin around so I'm now facing a wall of stone as I hang from the picks for dear life.

"I'm going down," I tell Trevor, who's now watching me from the position I was just in. His eyes are wide, pupils slightly dilated, though that could be the headlamp shining directly into them. He's definitely never been on a dig like this. He fancied himself Indiana Jones. It didn't occur to him I would be the hero in this story.

Okay, so this next part isn't very exciting. Show don't tell. I know, I know. But seriously, do you really want to hear about how I pull out one pick, move it down an inch or two, ram it back into the stone, and keep doing that over and over as my muscles burn and sweat drips down my face and pools under my arms, and in just about every other crack of my body? Yeah, it's not glamorous. If they make a movie, it'll be a lot more exciting, I'm sure. Until then, let's skip to the good part.

By the way, I totes want the young Lara Croft actress to play me, okay? She's a total badass. Now that we've got that handled...

My foot finally lands on something solid. This is where shit gets real. "You're almost there," I tell Trevor, who looks like he needs some encouragement. He only has one PhD, so, you know how it goes.

I'm just kidding about that. Most PhDs I know can't do this. Wouldn't want to do this. No matter how many they've collected. This is crazy. I'm crazy. But you probably figured that out already.

And Trevor isn't so bad. He's a product of his own privilege for sure, but then who isn't?

The key is some degree of self-awareness. Being woke, as they say. Trevor is anything but woke.

With both feet finally on solid ground, I exhale gratefully, letting my legs take more of my body's weight as I ease up on my arms. But I don't let go of my picks.

Not yet, anyway.

Why, you ask?

Clearly you've never been in a situation where the ground fell out from under your feet and the only things that saved your life were the climbing picks you held onto. But I don't hold that against you.

Even my closest friends think I'm total craycray.

So I hold on as I let more weight drop onto the floor beneath me. Another critter crunches under my boot. I feel no pity or remorse for its demise.

I pull one pick out of the stone while keeping hold of the other one with my right hand. "So far so good," I tell Trevor, who hasn't dared venture this close to the ground yet. "I'm going to let go and see if it holds."

"You sure about that?" he asks.

"Sure as I'll ever be."

And so I pull my other pick out but stay close to the stone wall, ready to slam my picks back into the rock the moment I feel the earth beneath me shift.

It doesn't. Hooray for me.

Carefully, I turn around to face the cavern.

I never know what to expect. Every discovery is different. Will this have monsters? Treasure? Dust bunnies? A little bit of each? It's anyone's guess.

This one is… empty.

Empty?

I squint, searching more carefully.

Yup. Empty.

Well, shit.

"Um, Trevor, we might have another problem."

He lowers himself next to me, still facing the wall. His

body is so close our shoulders brush against each other, and I wait to see if I feel that zing of attraction I felt before.

Nope. Fizzled already. Ah, well. These things never do last long.

"What problem?" he asks, breathless.

"See for yourself."

He turns slowly and then curses. "There's nothing here."

"That was my first thought too. But... we might be wrong." An idea is forming in my head. And so I slide my picks into their custom-made slots in my pants (what, yours don't have those?) and creep forward, into the center of the circular room. The wall reaches higher than I can see, with a great black emptiness above us. There are small crevices that break up the wall, like the one we snuck through, but otherwise it's giant and unending. The floor is a series of square stones in different shades of ochre and gray.

I find the center of the room and stand there, staring at my feet.

Trevor stays by the wall, presumably to be helpful, I'm sure. "See anything?" he asks, a nervous tremor in his voice.

Again, not judging, just reporting it like it is.

But I don't respond, because in fact, I do see something. The outline around the center stone is deeper and the grooves are more prominent compared to the rest of the floor. And that makes me wonder.

So I pace around it, my brain whirling, as pieces fall into place. Colors. Puzzles. Lines. Differences. Everything I observe clicking into a new order as I move the information around in my mind.

Until it snaps together and I laugh out loud. "Of course! Like in Budapest only with color."

"Budapest? What the hell are you going on about, Alex?"

I wave a hand at him dismissively and get to work, stepping on different stones in different configurations as I suss out the puzzle.

It takes time, but I am patient (oh, shut it. I am. When it counts.) Trevor paces impatiently (see, that's what it looks like to not be patient. Very different from *moi*, no?) Finally, I solve the riddle and jump back as the center stone begins to push itself up from the floor.

Under the stone is a compartment that holds the glowing fragment of what was once a perfect orb. But this is only a piece of the original orb. Global Tech thought they were getting the whole thing. Bam! Instant power. But I knew we would only find a piece.

How, you ask, could I possibly know that?

Because... I have one of the pieces. Shh... that's a secret no one but you and I know. I first discovered it after my parents were murdered when I was twelve. It was in a hidden vault under our Malibu mansion.

Which leaves a few more pieces out there. This is my life's work. This is what my parents died protecting and what I will risk my life to find.

I pull a canvas bag of rice out of my pocket. It happens to weigh exactly what this orb piece weighs. What an unlikely coincidence. Taking no chances—because of course I've seen Indiana Jones—I transfer the rice bag to the pedestal as I remove the orb, holding my breath and moving with cat-like grace.

When the transfer is complete, I look down in awe at the pulsing moon-like crevice slightly larger than my hand as the power it holds begins to pour through me. Closing my eyes, I open myself to its history.

Here's where I tell you my real secret. Promise you won't tell? Especially Mr. Wanna-Be-Jones here? Okay. Here it is.

I don't think I'm entirely human.

I mean, don't get me wrong. I look as human as they come. All the parts in all the appropriate places.

And I have the full range of human emotions.

But... I also can do things other humans can't.

Like read objects. I can touch an object and see its history. Where it's been. What it can do. What it's done.

It's my cheat. The reason I'm the best at what I do.

So, now you know. Hopefully we can still be friends. Cuz I dig you.

Get it? *Dig* you. Little archeology joke there.

So back to the orb. It's singing to me. Telling me its secrets. Showing me where I can find the last piece. But before I get the whole story, its voice is silenced.

As Trevor yanks it out of my hand.

I open my eyes and glare at him. "What the hell?"

He's now staring at it wide-eyed. "What makes it glow?"

"You know how rude that was?" I reach to take it back, but he pulls it away from me.

"Just give me a sec," he whines—and there is nothing more attractive than a grown man whining, am I right, ladies? "Besides, shouldn't you figure out a way out?"

Well, he's got a point there. If I rely on him, we'll die together in here, and I'm not spending the rest of my life— and all of my afterlife—with a one-night stand.

I glare at him a moment more, my instincts screaming at me to take the orb back and tuck it away safely where it belongs. But he's been working hard to find this thing, and I'm going to be ruining his career when I steal it from both him and Global Tech, so... whatever. I'll let him have his moment of glory.

As he said, I need to find a way out. Preferably one that doesn't require us scaling the wall we climbed down and crawling through the hall of bugs again.

I'm guessing there's another trick that will open a door.

So I study the tiles and put my thinking cap on. Meanwhile, Trevor's eyes are glued to the orb piece.

I have a lightbulb moment and wonder if it's too simple to work. But worth a try, am I right? I reverse my walk on the tiles that opened the secret compartment, and the middle tile returns into the ground. As it does, a piece of stone wall grinds against itself, peeling open a door that hadn't been there before.

Voila. We have an exit. I hold out my hand for the orb, and Trevor gives it back to me reluctantly then follows me to the door.

"Careful where you step," I say. "There are likely many booby traps still lurking around here."

"I'm not an idiot, Alex. I know what I'm doing."

Someone's getting testy. But I hold my tongue. See how diplomatic I can be? But of course, as he steps out of the chamber, pushing in front of me to do so, he nearly triggers said booby trap. One of the tiles is a different shade than the rest. I grab him and pull him back, then point. "That could have killed us," I tell him harshly, all patience wearing thin.

"You don't even know that's a trap," he says with more whine. Want any cheese with that, dude?

"Do you want to risk it when we're this close to getting out of here?"

He frowns at me. "Are we really that close?"

I nod and point down the corridor we just entered, showing him how this is where we started. "Just down that hall is the ladder we climbed down from the surface."

He smiles, and there's a glint in his eyes I don't like.

I don't see the knife in his hand until it's too late.

Until it's pushed into my gut. "Sorry about this, Alex. But I can't let you get all the credit, or turn this over to Global Tech. There are buyers willing to pay big for whatever this glowing bit is, and I intend to retire in wealth."

He pulls the artifact out of my pocket and pushes me backwards, onto the discolored tile I just warned him about.

Then he runs, coward that he is. He runs down the path I had to point out to him, while I fall, a knife sticking out of my gut. He makes it out just as my heel pushes on the tile unleashing the trap I knew was there.

Rushing water fills the cavern.

Oh joy. I love the suspense of how will Alex die today? Blood loss, internal injuries, or drowning?

Read it NOW.

ABOUT THE AUTHOR

Karpov Kinrade is the pen name for the husband and wife writing duo of USA TODAY bestselling, award-winning authors Lux Karpov-Kinrade and Dmytry Karpov-Kinrade.

Together, they write fantasy and science fiction novels and screenplays, make music and direct movies.

Look for more from Karpov Kinrade in *Vampire Girl, Of Dreams and Dragons, The Nightfall Chronicles* and *The Forbidden Trilogy*. If you're looking for their suspense and romance titles, you'll now find those under Alex Lux.

They live with their three mostly teens who share a

genius for all things creative, and six cats who think they rule the world (spoiler, they do.)

Find them online at KarpovKinrade.com

On Facebook /KarpovKinrade

On Twitter @KarpovKinrade

And subscribe to their newsletter for special deals and up-to-date notice of new launches.

~~~~~

If you enjoyed this book, consider supporting the author by leaving a review wherever you purchased this book. Thank you.

facebook.com/karpovkinrade

twitter.com/karpovkinrade

ALSO BY KARPOV KINRADE

In the Vampire Girl Universe

Vampire Girl

Vampire Girl 2: Midnight Star

Vampire Girl 3: Silver Flame

Vampire Girl 4: Moonlight Prince

Vampire Girl 5: First Hunter

Vampire Girl 6: Unseen Lord

Vampire Girl 7: Fallen Star

Vampire Girl: Copper Snare

Vampire Girl: Crimson Cocktail

Vampire Girl: Christmas Cognac

Of Dreams and Dragons

Moonstone Academy (a new series coming 2019)

Ellabelle: A Moonstone Academy Prequel Novella

The Nightfall Chronicles

Made in United States
Orlando, FL
25 August 2024

50766734R00098